EMILY AND THE SPELLSTONE

EMILY
AND THE
SPELLSTONE

MICHAEL RUBENS

CLARION BOOKS

HOUGHTON MIFFLIN HARCOURT

BOSTON NEW YORK

Clarion Books, 3 Park Avenue, New York, New York 10016

Clarion Books is an imprint of Houghton Mifflin Harcourt Publishing Company.

www.hmhco.com

The text was set in Dante MT.

Design by Lisa Vega

Library of Congress Cataloging-in-Publication Data

Names: Rubens, Michael, author.

Title: Emily and the Spellstone / Michael Rubens.

Description: Boston ; New York : Clarion Books, 2017. | Summary: Twelve-year-old Emily accidentally releases Gorgo, a carnivorous demon, from the magic Spellstone to which he is bound, and must join him in protecting the Stone from villains planning world domination.

Identifiers: LCCN 2016025962 | ISBN 9780544790865 (hardback)

Subjects: | CYAC: Adventure and adventurers—Fiction. | Magic—Fiction. | Demonology—Fiction. | Stones—Fiction. | Friendship—Fiction. | BISAC: JUVENILE FICTION / Fantasy & Magic. | JUVENILE FICTION / Action & Adventure / General. | JUVENILE FICTION / Humorous Stories. | JUVENILE FICTION / Social Issues / Friendship.

Classification: LCC PZ7.R8295 Emi 2017 | DDC [Fic]—dc23

LC record available at https://lccn.loc.gov/2016025962

Manufactured in the United States of America

DOC 10 9 8 7 6 5 4 3 2 1

4500655038

For Minya,

who found the Stone

EMILY AND THE SPELLSTONE

CHAPTER
ONE

It was **Emily Edelman's twelfth birthday.**

It was a fateful day.

Fateful because she was about to find something very rare and *very* powerful.

And that very rare and powerful something would launch Emily on a great adventure — "great" in this case meaning "absurdly dangerous" — that would profoundly change her life.

Most likely by . . . well . . . ending it. Horribly.

But let's not get ahead of ourselves.

At this point, Emily didn't know about any of that.

What she did know was that it was a *perfect* day: The sky was perfectly blue, the sun perfectly warm, the clouds perfectly fluffy; the sand was perfectly soft, the ocean waves perfectly wave-y.

And she was in a perfectly awful, perfectly black mood.

Why? Where to start . . .

You could start with her big sister, Hilary, who was driving her insane. Or her obnoxious little brother, Dougie, who was driving her insaner, which Emily knew wasn't a real word but felt accurate.

Or you could start with the fact that she'd been at her new school for only a week, and already everyone despised her. Especially some girl named Kristy Meyer, who was beautiful and popular and for some reason went out of her way to be mean to Emily.

"I'm pretty sure you're imagining it," said Mrs. Edelman, Emily's mother.

Emily was pretty sure she wasn't.

When her father had told her he'd been transferred and they were moving across the country, Emily said she didn't *want* to move because she'd never see her friends again, and she *liked* where they lived, and it would be *awful*. But her father said, "Aw, c'mon! We'll be living near the ocean! It will be fun! It will be an adventure!"

"I *hate* adventures," Emily replied.

He said, "I'm pretty sure you don't really mean that."

Emily was pretty sure she did.

That was another thing that was driving her crazy:

the way her parents were always so *sure* that Emily didn't know anything, even the things that were going on inside her own head. Like she was still a baby. When Emily said she hated adventures, she knew what she was talking about.

Adventure, she had learned, was an adult code word that actually meant "disruption and discomfort and change," none of which Emily was partial to. Last year in school the students had had to create personal profiles. Under hobbies Emily put *hibernating* and *collecting rocks. Hibernating* because Emily's idea of an ideal evening was to wrap herself up in a cozy blanket and read a book (preferably one without too much adventure). *Collecting rocks* because she had a vague affection for geology: it was for the most part stable and slow-moving and trustworthy and comforting.

What else was bothering her? How about their new house, which turned out to be a very *old* house that made weird noises and smelled bad. "Doesn't it have great character?" her mom kept repeating. "Doesn't it?" Then got upset when Emily finally blurted, "Sure does! Old and smelly!"

Plus Emily got the worst bedroom, *plus* the box with her agate collection had gone missing in the move, *plus* her hamster had dropped dead right before they left, probably of a broken heart, and *plus* she didn't even want to come to the beach today to celebrate her birthday. But what did her parents say? "Sure you do!"

Plus plus *plus:* The one gift she had asked for—the *one single thing*—she didn't get. And why?

"OOOooOOoh."

Because of her older sister, Hilary.

"OOOooooOOOoohhh."

That was Hilary right now, sitting across from Emily on the picnic blanket, moaning piteously.

"Hilary," said their mother sharply, "give me that phone!"

Mrs. Edelman put down her own phone so she could snatch the phone away from Hilary, who was futilely attempting to text, groaning in agony with each letter.

This was why Emily didn't get the only thing she'd asked for.

A minor scuffle broke out as Mrs. Edelman tried to take the device, Hilary's bejeweled phone case shedding rhinestones in the process. Six-year-old Dougie, momentarily distracted from scooping sand into Emily's uneaten sandwich when she wasn't looking, giggled.

"Give it to me!" said their mother to Hilary. "Where did you get it?!"

"But, *Mommmmm*," moaned Hilary, who was fifteen,

"I have to text Cassie because she's breaking up with Kyle, and Jennie said she's talking with Brad, and Kerry is—"

"I don't care!" snapped their mother. "I thought I had locked this in my desk drawer! Edward," she said to their father, "did you see what she's been doing?"

Mr. Edelman looked up from *his* phone. "Hilary," he said, "you know the doctor said you have to take a break!"

He had indeed. The doctor's stern, doom-laden instructions—and Hilary's groans of pain—stemmed from Hilary's current condition, which stemmed from Hilary's terrible addiction to the mobile phone she had received for *her* birthday. Despite her fervent promises to the contrary, she had devoted so much time online and texting her friends—most of her waking hours, really—that she had suddenly developed a whole collection of crippling physical ailments. Not only did she now require glasses to focus beyond a distance of two feet, but she had to undertake a punishing course of physical therapy just to be able to hold her head in a normal upright position. But the worst were her thumbs, which were now encased in soft casts to help their overexerted joints recover.

So when Emily had said to her parents, "The only

single thing that I want for my birthday is a phone and you don't have to get me anything else and all my friends are getting them and I just want to be able to contact them and I promise I'll have more self-control than Hilary and I'm old enough," they said, "We're pretty sure you're not."

Argh.

After her mom had successfully pried the phone from Hilary's hands, she shook it at Emily and said, "This is why you're not getting a phone. You are way too young!" As if Hilary's behavior was all Emily's fault.

So, sitting there on the beach on a perfect day on her twelfth birthday, Emily was feeling alone, lonely, friendless, dislocated, discomfited, deprived, and unfairly treated like a child. She didn't know that very soon she'd look back fondly on these problems and think, *Ah, if only I could go back to that time . . .*

But for now, it was all awful. Gazing out toward the waves, she reached distractedly for her sandwich and took a bite.

"AUUGHPTTTTTHHHH!! DOUGIE!"

So there was another patch of excitement and shouting, from which Dougie somehow emerged without any real punishment. LIKE ALWAYS.

When that was over and Emily had managed to rinse most of the sand out of her mouth with lemonade, her father said, "Cheer up, sweetie—wait till you see the cake I got you!"

Beaming with pride, he opened the box and presented it to her.

Emily saw what was written on it, clapped both hands to her forehead, and said, "Glrrrbb."

"'Happy eleventh birthday,'" she muttered darkly. "'Happy *eleventh* birthday!'"

Emily angrily upended another bucket of sand to add to the castle she was creating, far down the beach from where her family was.

That's what the cake had said, in big, happy letters:

HAPPY ELEVENTH BIRTHDAY, EMILY!

They didn't even know she was *twelve!*

When her father had opened the box, Emily had said "Glrrrbb," because that sound, emerging through gritted teeth, is the sound you create when you strangle a scream.

HAPPY ELEVENTH BIRTHDAY, EMILY!

Argh.

Her family, of course, thought the whole thing was

hysterical. Her parents laughed. Dougie brayed like a donkey. Even Hilary, whose interactions with the family mostly consisted of her rolling her eyes, joined in the laughter.

"It's not funny!" said Emily.

"Actually," said Hilary, "it's *really* funny."

"Sweetie," said her father, "I'm sorry. The bakery must have screwed it up."

"Uh-huh," said Emily. "How do you explain that candle?"

Her father took a better look at what he was placing on the cake—one of those candles in the shape of a number. Which, in this case, was 11.

Her father stared at the candle, as if trying to comprehend exactly what he was looking at. Then he said: "HA HA HA HA HAAAA!"

. . . and the rest of the family joined in again.

"Stop laughing!" said Emily.

"Honey, come on," said her mother. "We all know that you're . . . uh . . ."

"TWELVE!"

"Of course! Let's all just sing 'Happy Birthday' and enjoy the cake. Come on, everyone. 'Haaaappy biiiirthday to—'" which is when the seagull pooped on the cake and everyone burst into hysterical laughter again and Emily bellowed, "That's IT! I've HAD IT!" and stormed off down the beach.

It shouldn't surprise her that they didn't know how old she was, she thought as she built up the castle. She was lucky they put an eleven on the cake—most of the time they treated her as though she were the same age as Dougie.

Dougie. Ugh-y Dougie. Not for the first time she flashed through a quick fantasy of him being conveniently abducted by aliens. Conveniently and *permanently*.

"He's just being rambunctious," her parents always said.

Rambunctious. That made it sound *cute*. *Obnoxious* was the correct word, a word that would describe the sort of kid who—

"AAARGH, I'M A GIANT MONSTER!!!"

—who would rudely interrupt the narrator mid-sentence and trample your sandcastle and then run off down the beach giggling before you even had a chance to shout, "DOUGIE!!!"

"That's IT!" said Emily again, looking at her ruined sandcastle. "I've HAD IT!" She was aware that she had declared that that was *IT* and she'd *HAD IT* and stormed off down the beach once before, but this time it was *really* true, and so she stormed off even *farther* down the beach.

Toward her destiny. The one mentioned at the beginning of the chapter. The one that will almost certainly lead to her destruction.

Emily was wandering along the edge of the water, picking up and examining the small stones and pebbles strewn on the wet sand: "Hmm. Igneous. Interesting," or "Quartz. Perfect." The best ones she placed in a little plastic bucket. As she collected rocks she continued muttering to herself: "Stupid family. Stupid new school. Stupid Kristy Meyer . . ." She came upon a small puddle of seawater left over from the high tide and spotted her reflection in it: frizzy hair like her mother, which Emily hated; a slightly too-big nose like her father, which Emily also hated. She stuck out her tongue at herself— "Stupid me!"—and moved on.

Then she saw it.

It was ahead of her, halfway sunken in the wet sand, appearing and disappearing under a few inches of water each time a wave came in.

She crouched down and picked it up.

It was a stone, the most curiously shaped stone

Emily had ever seen: weirdly rectangular and flat, a light grayish-brown, maybe half an inch thick. Its form, although rough and irregular, reminded her of nothing so much as a cell phone.

The thought made her laugh grimly. "I'm getting a phone after all," she said out loud.

And right then she had the strangest sensation: that the stone vibrated briefly in her hand, as if in friendly recognition. *Hello,* the stone seemed to say. *There you are!* And in that same brief moment—no more than the time it took for the next wave to arrive and spread itself over the shoreline and cover her feet—it seemed a voice spoke to Emily, a voice without words, filling her mind with rather unsettling thoughts of distant lands and pro- found mysteries and perilous exploits. And of power.

Then the wave receded and the moment was over.

Emily stood stock-still, barely breathing, staring at the stone, wondering if she had imagined it. Everything was normal. The seagulls squawked. The waves made their gentle crashing noises.

It had been like a poem, she thought. Or no, like a song. Or the feeling you get when you hear a song. And there was something else. Something . . . a little scary. She could have sworn that she had heard *another* voice, hidden away beneath the songless song: a cheerful voice, yes, but not at all friendly. A voice that spoke actual words.

What it had said, she thought, was, *"I can't wait to eat you."*

"Whaddya got? Whaddisit! Gimme it! Lemme see!"

Dougie grabbed at the stone, snapping Emily out of her reverie.

"Dougie! Leggo! That's mine!" She pulled the stone out of his reach, twisting and turning to keep it away from him as he snatched at it, the odd experience already forgotten.

"Kids!" Her father, calling to them from down the beach, waving for them to come back. "Time to go!"

"C'mon," said Dougie. "Lemme just see it!"

"Dougie, no!" she said. She wasn't sure why she cared that much, but he was *not* getting this stone. "Here," she said, shoving the bucket full of rocks at him. "You can have these." Emily started tromping back toward her parents.

The stone felt warm in her hand.

That night in her new bedroom that she didn't like in the new old house that she also didn't like, Emily sat on her bed and examined the stone curiously, tracing its surface with her fingertips. She wasn't sure what sort of stone it was—maybe metamorphic, she thought, squeezed into its unusual shape by unimaginable heat and pressure deep in the earth, eons and eons ago. This time she didn't hear or feel anything: no unsung song, no voices either friendly or threatening.

"You're just a rock," she said out loud.

"Emily, bedtime," said her mom from the hallway. "Lights out."

"Okay."

She placed the flat stone on her windowsill, climbed back into bed, and turned off the lamp on her nightstand. She was soon asleep.

The stone lay on her windowsill in a patch of moonlight.

Gaining power.

CHAPTER
TWO

Perhaps nothing would have happened. Perhaps Emily would have continued living a very normal life, instead of being propelled toward her probably fatal fate. Except for her mother.

"You did *what?!*" Emily said at breakfast.

"I've signed you up for the class talent show," repeated her mother. "I was talking to Mr. Petersen next door, and he suggested it. I didn't even know until yesterday that he's your drama teacher."

It was true—balding, nervous, cardigan-sweater-wearing Mr. Petersen, the drama teacher, was their next-door neighbor. Emily had learned this with a certain amount of horror. Teachers were not supposed to exist outside of school, much less live next door to you.

"He seems like a *very* nice man," her mother added.

"Mom, how could you sign me up without even *asking* me?"

"Honey, it's the perfect way to meet people. You've been complaining that you don't have any friends here."

"No, I've been complaining that everyone here *hates* me!"

"I'm pretty sure that's not true."

In this case, Emily's mother was right. Or sort of right. It was a bit more complicated than everyone hating Emily. It had to do with Kristy Meyer.

Kristy Meyer hated Emily. And that was enough.

So. Kristy Meyer.

If you looked through last year's yearbook from Clearview School, you'd see lots of pictures of Kristy, partially because she made sure she was on the yearbook committee. Look, there she is, smiling and waving from a family vacation at a luxury resort in the Caribbean. There she is, holding a gymnastics trophy. There she is, in very expensive English riding gear, riding a very expensive horse. And there she is, winner in not one but *two* superlative categories: *Prettiest* and *Most Likely to Become President.*

Some unknown student had managed to hack into the yearbook file and alter the award categories so they read *Most Likely to Be Randomly Vicious to You for Absolutely No Reason* and *Most Likely to Become a Horrible Dictator.*

The school had had to reprint several hundred copies of the yearbook and tried to recall the hacked versions. But there were still copies floating around, and the students at Clearview who weren't part of Kristy's clique would secretly pass around the original copies and giggle.

Early on, Kristy had learned what she felt was an important lesson: One way to get friends was to be pleasant and compassionate and generally nice to everyone. But that method was a lot of work and not much fun. It was much easier—and more fun—to just be nice to *certain* people (that is, people who were as attractive and wealthy as you), while being generally dismissive of *most* people and *really mean* to *some* of them. That way her group of friends—the *right* people, really—always had targets to unite against. Those friends were also terrified of falling out of favor with her, because they knew that then she'd be mean to *them.* And the rest of the students were terrified of her as well. So people fell into line.

But it always helped to have fresh meat. And to Kristy, Emily was the perfect target. She was new, meaning that she was defenseless. She was quiet. She had frizzy hair and seemed somewhat confused about which clothes were cool and which weren't. And what else? Actually, the first two items—*new* and *defenseless*—were more than enough for Kristy.

Emily met Kristy within the first ten minutes of the very first day of school. Kristy approached her, surrounded by her friends (all of whom, Emily noted, had their own phones and were busily texting, probably one another, Emily thought bitterly). Things Kristy did *not* say: "Hi! Are you new?" or "Where are you from?" or "Hi, I'm Kristy! Welcome to Clearview School!" No. The first thing she said was, "Where did you get that shirt?"

Emily looked down at her shirt. It was a black T-shirt with a sort of skull-and-crossbones/guitar pattern on it. She liked it. She looked back up at Kristy, who was waiting expectantly, her arms crossed, chin up. Kristy was smiling. It wasn't a nice smile.

"Uh, hi, I'm Emily?" said Emily.

"You're the new girl," said Kristy. She said it in a way that suggested that this was automatically something bad.

"Yyyyyes," said Emily. She examined the other girls. You had to give Kristy credit: She didn't care about your skin color or things like that. The girls behind Kristy were an inspiringly diverse group, united by a shared belief in their own good looks, money, the right clothes, and being nasty to others.

"Why are you wearing a boy's shirt?" asked Kristy.

"It's my cousin's. He's a boy. I like this shirt."

The other girls giggled.

"I can't believe you'd wear a boy's shirt," said Kristy.

"I guess I don't care so much about that stuff," said Emily. "Nice to meet you." She turned and walked away, the other girls exchanging delighted OMG expressions and giggling more.

Perfect, thought Kristy.

Over the next few days, in her mysterious manner, she made it known that there was *something wrong* with Emily. Just a few carefully selected words here, a raised eyebrow there, a smirk at the right moment. No one knew exactly *how,* but it came to be understood—in the same way that everyone understands that the sky is blue—that there was *something wrong* with the new girl and she should be avoided. It's not so much that kids actually disliked her—how could they? No one knew her. It's just that no one wanted to risk being the first to stand up and say, *Wait a second . . .*

So when Emily said, "Everyone here *hates* me," she

was wrong. It had nothing to do with her specifically. Everyone was just afraid to be her friend.

Her mother's strategy of volunteering her for the talent show *might* have helped. That is, if Kristy Meyer wasn't also in the talent show.

The rehearsals were every day after school for almost a week. When Emily showed up for the first day, she thought, *Oh, no . . .*

Kristy was there, smirking at her. "You're doing the talent show?" she said to Emily. "How . . . great."

Mr. Petersen oversaw the rehearsals. To Emily he seemed like a very nice and well-intentioned man, but also the sort who, if you were building a set, would accidentally drop a hammer onto his foot and stumble into a bucket of paint and staple-gun his sleeve to a wall. All of which he did during the rehearsals.

He said to Emily, "And what sort of act would you like to do?"

"Um . . . nothing?" suggested Emily.

"How about a magic trick?"

"Uh . . ."

"Wonderful!"

And so it was decided that she would do a magic trick. He gave her a black velvet bag. It had a secret compartment.

"You put something in it," he said enthusiastically, putting an apple into the bag, "and when you take it out, *behold!* It's . . . *different!*"

Emily looked at the orange Mr. Petersen was now holding.

"Amazing, right?" he said.

"Amazing," she said, to be polite.

"Wonderful. Here, take it. I have to work on the lighting and music cues for Kristy's act—it's gonna be another spectacular one."

Kristy smirked at Emily again.

And that's how the week went. Kristy did not have to say a further word to Emily. But she was an expert smirker. A *surgical* smirker. Emily came to almost respect the skill of that smirk. Kristy was also brilliant at innocently whispering or exchanging glances or texting with other girls, while somehow making it clear to Emily that the whispers and glances and texts were about her.

At rehearsal, each kid would dutifully present an act—songs, a monologue or two, other magic tricks. Kristy's act involved simultaneously spinning several batons while doing complicated acrobatics. When Mr. Petersen coached everyone, he would say things like

"Smile more!" and "Engage the audience!" and especially "Watch how Kristy does it!"

During the day, Emily went from class to class, the other students treating her as if she didn't exist. Very soon she'd be wishing they were still ignoring her. But she didn't know that.

At dinner one night, Mrs. Edelman said, "How are rehearsals going? Are you getting to know the other kids?"

"I sure am," said Emily.

"Great!" said her mother. "We're all so excited to see it this Thursday! Right, kids?"

"So excited," said Hilary, with an evil grin.

And so the stage was set for Thursday, the evening of the performance, raising the curtain on what could be the dramatic final act for Emily.

In hindsight, Emily realized her big mistake was deciding not to just stick with an apple and an orange for her trick, the way Mr. Petersen had. No, she just *had* to use the stone.

The morning of the performance, just before leaving for school, her eyes had fallen upon the stone sitting on her windowsill.

Use me, it had said.

"What?" Emily said.

She hadn't *heard* anything, exactly. But it was like that day on the beach, the strange sense that the stone was somehow reaching out to her.

Use me.

Emily shook her head. She was imagining it. But now that you mentioned it, why *not* use the stone? Instead of changing an apple into an orange—*booooring*—why not change the stone, she thought, into an actual phone? Stone to phone. Phone stone. Stone phone.

Her father had a shoebox of old, broken phones that he had never bothered to dispose of and that had somehow survived the move. Emily had played with them when she was younger. Dougie still did. She could use one of them: *Behold this ancient stone. I put it in this bag, and when I take it out, Zowie McWowie! It's turned into a real mobile phone!*

So that's what she had with her right now as she stood offstage in the wings, gnawing her nails with anxiety: the velvet bag, an old cell phone, and the stone. Onstage a boy named Lewis was doing violence to a Beatles song. In the audience, parents smiled indulgent if rather rigid smiles. Younger siblings squirmed. Older siblings yawned. Emily knew that her family was out there, even though she had begged them not to come.

"This is gonna be awful," whispered Hilary now.

"Shh!" said their mother.

Backstage, the other performers milled about. Kristy Meyer had on a red, white, and blue outfit covered with glittering sequins. Emily watched her rehearse a front flip, land it perfectly, and manage a 10.0 smirk at Emily at the same time.

Onstage, Lewis's voice cracked in a particularly penetrating manner.

Emily decided to go to the soundproof rehearsal room.

The room was right off the backstage area. It was big enough for a small band to practice in, the walls lined with black acoustic insulation that had the bumpy pattern of egg cartons.

Once inside, Emily closed the heavy door, thankful that it blocked out Lewis's caterwauling. She laid out the phone, the stone, and the black velvet bag on a small table. She didn't really feel like practicing, but at least it might help distract her from her nervousness. So she picked up the velvet bag and put the real cell phone into the secret compartment.

"Behold this simple bag," she said to her invisible audience. "Note that there is nothing inside it."

She held the bag open and swung it back and forth to display its apparent lack of contents.

"And now behold this simple stone," she said, raising it in one hand. "I shall now perform an amazing act of transformation. I will place the stone in this empty bag, and, activating the ancient occult powers granted me by my inalienable birthright as a Stonemaster—"

At this point Emily paused and raised her eyebrows, surprised and rather impressed by her last sentence, which had just sort of appeared in her mind.

"—and exercising that birthright, I hereby initiate and awaken this stone!"

She hadn't prepared *that*, either, but she had to admit that it sounded pretty good. With a flourish, she placed the stone into the bag and closed it.

"And . . . *behold!*" she said, plunging her hand back into the bag and triumphantly removing the real cell phone, feeling a much greater thrill than she had expected.

Oh, that was a surprise. The phone was switched on, the screen glowing. Maybe it wasn't broken after all. Well, that would certainly make the trick better if— *wait a second*.

"What the . . . ?" said Emily.

She scrunched and unscrunched her eyes in case they were playing tricks on her. She held the phone closer to her face and then farther away. She tilted her hand back and forth and did more eye scrunching and shook her head.

None of that helped.

No matter what she did, it wasn't the phone she was holding. It was the *stone.* But one surface was now alive and glowing, very much like the screen on a phone, except this seemed to have much more *depth* to it, as if she were peering through a window into an infinite pale blue void that was gently churning and changing. Once again she had the mysterious sensation she had felt on the beach, that of great power.

"Wha . . . ?"

As she stared at the glowing rectangle in wonder, a series of objects began to materialize and drift around within it.

"I can*not* believe this," Emily breathed.

The objects were similar to what you would see on any mobile smartphone: icons and little images for different apps. But these floating images gave a sense of realness, of incredible detail and three dimensions, as if Emily could reach into the glowing screen and pick up one of the little moving objects and roll it around between her thumb and forefinger. There were all sorts of items: things that looked like miniature but very alive versions of mythical beasts; tiny castles; a tree that appeared to be absolutely real; an ancient-looking parchment map; a full moon that slowly rotated in the upper right-hand corner of the screen . . .

Emily didn't feel afraid. She felt mesmerized. And also as if she were trying to recall something very important that hovered just at the edge of her memory. As for the talent show, she had completely forgotten about that.

Moving in dreamlike slow motion, she reached out a finger to touch the tiny objects that hovered in front of her. But as she did so, something came zooming up from the far distance, growing rapidly in size until it filled the screen, crowding out everything else.

It appeared to be a stone urn—ancient, roughly made. Symbols were carved onto the sides—runes, maybe?

For the first time, Emily felt a low hum of fear.

As though there was something dangerous about the urn. The runes themselves were unpleasant— something spidery and threatening about them. And as she looked at them, they rearranged themselves into a single word:

FREE

Somehow Emily knew that the runes hadn't done any rearranging—her brain had done the rearranging, translating the runes for her.

Despite her growing sense of unease, she found herself reaching out to touch the floating urn. She gasped. It *was* real. She picked it up. It was about the size of a bottle of nail polish. It had weight.

It was then that she noticed another word. Written under "FREE" in much smaller runes was

ME

"'Free me'?" she said.

Part of her, some deep-down part, was screaming, *Replace the urn! Put it back! Don't touch it!* The same way you wouldn't click on a link in a suspicious email that promised you millions of dollars. *And most of all,* said her mind, *do not read out loud what the urn says on the back!*

Still moving as if in a dream, Emily turned the urn around and saw more runes, runes that again she was somehow able to read.

"Abra . . ." she said, "ka . . . donkulous?"

Then it seemed as if the urn was exploding in flames and the whole room was filled with darkness and smoke and she fell backwards and when she opened her eyes it was *worse* because there was a giant creature in front of her, a demon, she thought, a *demon,* and the demon grinned with his mouth full of gleaming predatory teeth and bellowed, "I AM GOING TO EAT YOU!!"

Emily screamed.

CHAPTER
THREE

The thing about soundproof rooms is, they're sound-proof. Especially when there is, say, music thumping loudly outside. And there was. Kristy Meyer had just taken the stage to the music she had selected, strutting out from the wings with perfect poise and grace, twirling her batons so fast they were humming blurs. She did a double pirouette. The audience oohed. She did a no-handed walkover. The audience aahed.

"Wow—she's really something, isn't she?" said Mrs. Edelman to Mr. Edelman.

In the wings, Mr. Petersen was smiling proudly as Kristy hurled her batons into the air, did a backflip, and caught them both.

Aaahh, said everyone again, and applauded.

Mr. Petersen looked around to make sure Emily was

ready to go on. *Poor kid*, he thought. *She's going to have to follow this stellar act. Now, where is she?*

Where she was: cowering in abject terror in a corner of the soundproof rehearsal room, a gigantic man-shaped demon or demon-shaped man advancing upon her.

"I AM GOING TO EAT YOU!" he thundered again, his third thundering of that phrase, and the single thing he had thundered so far. Emily screamed again, the only sound *she* had managed to make.

He was nearly as tall as the room, wider than the door. His muscular body was grayish green and covered with spikes and bumps like you'd find on a desert lizard. He was wearing some sort of pants that were shredded below his knees. His eyes were burning yellow. His hands ended in wickedly curved talons. And his teeth . . .

And then there was the fire. Little spurts of flame kept erupting here and there on his body as if he were volcanically active. When he roared, flames jetted from his mouth. There were flames coming from his *armpits*, for goodness' sake.

"HA HA HA!" he flame-laughed. "I AM GOING TO EAT YOU!" And he stooped and reached out to seize her.

Just as she felt his claws on her skin, she screamed, "WAIT!"

He froze, leaning forward, the claw still entrapping her.

He didn't move.

Emily didn't move.

Her heart pounded so hard she thought surely she would die.

He still didn't move.

And did some more not moving.

Then she saw his eyes dart to the side for a moment, then back to her.

"Uh . . ." he said. "Now what?"

"EEEEEEEEEE!!!" Emily screamed. The demon jumped.

"HELP ME!" screamed Emily. "Heeeelp! HEEEEELP!"

The demon was holding his massive hands over his pointed ears.

"HEEEEELP!!!"

"Hold *on!*" he said. "How? What do you want?"

"Help!"

"I know! I know! How!? *How* am I supposed to help you?"

"HEEEELLLL—what?" said Emily.

"You said, 'Help.' How. Do. You. Want. Me. To. Help. You?"

Emily stared at him, shaking. Her breath was coming in ragged gasps.

"What are you talking about?" she finally said. "Why did you keep saying you were going to eat me?"

"I couldn't think of anything else to say! I've been imprisoned in that stone for an eternity, and suddenly I'm out, and it was the first thing that popped into my head!"

"So you're *not* going to eat me?"

"No! I mean, yes! I mean, I'd *like* to, I fully *intend* to, but . . . I *have* to help you!"

Emily did a few more moments of staring.

"You *have* to *help* me?"

"Yes! I'm . . ." Here the creature appeared to undergo some sort of internal struggle, as if he—or it—was trying to prevent himself—or itself—from saying something vitally important that he—or it, you get the point—didn't want to say.

"I'm . . . I'm . . . *I'm bound to your service and have to obey you!*" he blurted. "Argh! Ahhh!" he said, and slammed his giant palm into his gigantic forehead several times. "Why"—*slam*—"did I have"—*slam slam*—"to tell her that?" *Slam slam slam.*

Emily unsteadily got to her feet, her back pressed against the wall. "Who are you?" she said, because of the several hundred questions she had, that seemed like a good place to start.

The demon drew himself up to his full height.

"I am Baelmadeus Gorgostopheles Lacrimagnimum Turpisatos Metuotimo Dolorosum Tenebris Morsitarus."

To Emily it sounded like one long, many-syllabled word.

"Baelma—?" she started.

"Just call me Gorgo. That's what my friends call me."

"You have friends?"

He considered this for a moment. "Nnnno."

"Are you a . . . demon?"

"Whoa, whoa, whoa. Easy on the pejoratives, okay?"

"The what-atives?"

"The unpleasant names!"

"You're *not* a demon?"

"Would you *please*? I'd prefer if you'd just think of me as a nearly immortal creature of evil intent with powers that you can't even imagine. Who can bench-press a *lot*."

He flexed. Emily believed him.

"And *you* have to obey *me*?" said Emily.

"Yes! Until such time as I'm freed by some trick or

power, at which point I will consume you! But until then I have to serve you."

"How?"

"What do you mean, how? However. Do you have enemy armies that need smiting? Castle walls destroyed and the habitations put to flame? A mountain moved?"

"Um . . . can you do math?"

"Wha?"

"How about wishes? Can you grant wishes?"

"Do I look like a genie to you?"

"How would I know?"

"What are you talking about?" said Gorgo. "How can someone so ignorant be a Stonemaster?"

The stone. The stone! She'd forgotten all about it. It was lying face-up on the floor, still glowing.

"What *is* that?" she said, pointing to it.

Gorgo seemed stunned. "You don't *know?* It's a *Stone.*"

He said it in such a way that the capital letter was obvious.

"A stone?"

"No, a *Stone.* It's one of the most powerful objects in the multiverse. It's a device, shall we say, for the working of the greatest thaumaturgies. That is," he added, looking at Emily sideways, "in the correct hands."

"Thauma-whaties?"

"Hoo boy. Like I said, in the correct hands."

There was a knocking on the door.

"Emily?" It was Mr. Petersen, his voice faint because of the acoustic insulation. "Emily, are you in there?"

"Another person!" said Gorgo. "I'm going to eat him, too!"

"No!" said Emily. "No eating anyone!"

"What?!"

"Just a minute, Mr. Petersen!" she said.

"I can't eat *anyone*?"

"No! That's an order!" she said, although she did think briefly about Kristy.

"Is everything okay?" said Mr. Petersen.

"All good! I'm just changing!"

"You're almost on!"

"Okay!"

"Why do I smell smoke?" said Mr. Petersen. "Can I come in?"

"Hold on!" she called in the direction of the door. "Quick!" she said to Gorgo. "Hide!"

"Okay! How's this?"

He was now crouching down behind a music stand, which didn't do much to hide him because (a) even crouching down he was taller than Emily, and

(b) it was a music stand and couldn't have hidden a three-year-old.

"That's not working at all."

"Okay, can I hide behind you?"

Emily blinked at him. "You have to get back in the stone," she said.

"I told you, it's a *Stone*."

"Whatever! Get in there!"

"I just got out!"

"But you *can* go back in, can't you?"

"Yes, but it's not the same as before. I won't fit the same way!"

"Emily, I'm opening the door!" said Mr. Petersen.

"Too bad!" she said to Gorgo. "Get in there right now!"

Gorgo sighed, rolled his eyes, and muttered something to himself. Then, just as the rehearsal door was opening, Gorgo suddenly folded himself in half *backwards*, and then that half folded again, and so on, a rapid bit of occult origami, until he had become a small package that hopped itself up and into the Stone as if it were jumping into a pool. And just like that, Gorgo was gone.

Emily darted to the Stone, snatched it up off the floor, and held the glowing side against her stomach just as Mr. Petersen entered the room.

"Emily, are you okay?"

"Yes, I'm fine!"

"I thought I heard screaming in here."

"It's just part of my act. I was practicing."

"I see. Have you been lighting something on fire? It smells like smoke in here."

"Does it?"

"Your act doesn't have any fire in it, right?"

"No, nothing."

A muffled voice said, "Ugh, this is *so* uncomfortable."

"What?" said Mr. Petersen.

"Nothing!"

"Well, hurry up and get out there — you've got about thirty seconds until Kristy is done. By the way — she's *amazing*."

"Great."

As Mr. Petersen escorted her firmly across the backstage area, Emily said, "Mr. Petersen, I really don't think I can go out there."

"Nonsense," he said. "You'll be fine. It's just stage fright."

"No, Mr. Petersen, you don't understand," she said, but he was already steering her toward the wings.

"Get out there!"

The audience saw Emily make her entrance—or, more accurately, have her entrance made for her—as she came stumbling onstage from the wings as if she had been given a *very* encouraging push.

"Oh, look, there she is!" said Mrs. Edelman excitedly.

"Oh, look, there she goes," said Mr. Edelman.

And indeed, Emily was trying to return to the wings. Now Mr. Petersen's hands were visible, gesturing vigorously to her to stay out there. Emily turned to the audience with a dazed expression that said, *Oh my goodness, those headlights are coming right at me.* The audience chuckled, but it was a nervous chuckle, as if they wanted to believe that this was part of the act but weren't sure.

Dougie whispered loudly, "What is she doing? Is this supposed to be funny?" neatly summing up the question in everyone's mind.

From the Stone, Emily heard Gorgo say, "What's going on?"

"Be quiet!" she said, a bit too loud, and the chuckling from the audience stopped.

"*Oh. Em. Gee.* She's totally tanking," said her sister. "This is *so* embarrassing."

"Shh!" said their mother.

Emily looked out at the audience. They stared back in total silence. Her mother waved at her. Her brother was wide-eyed with fascination. Her sister was slouched down, a hand covering her face.

"I'm sorry, ladies and gentlemen, but I just discovered that this rock I found on the beach is a magic Stone and there was a demon who isn't a demon but is *like* a demon trapped inside and he says he plans to eat me but for now he's my servant and this all happened a minute ago and so I'm feeling just a *little* delicate and confused so if you'll excuse me I think I'll just go lie down in a dark room for a few days."

Is what she *wanted* to say, and very nearly did. But didn't. Instead she stood there saying nothing.

"Oh, boy," sighed her father. Her sister sank down even farther in her seat.

From the Stone came a few grunts and mutters, the sound someone trapped in a box might make as he shifted around, trying to find a more comfortable position. Emily hoped the people in the front row couldn't hear it.

She looked to her right. Mr. Petersen was still in the wings, nodding manically at her, his eyes wide. "Start! Start!" he mouthed. She looked the other way. There was Kristy Meyer, smirking at her.

Well, forget *that,* thought Emily.

"L-ladies and gentlemen," she said, her voice quiet

and shaky. She cleared her throat and tried again, more forcefuly this time. "Ladies and gentlemen!"

At that moment she heard the loud and unmistakable sound of a belch.

The audience heard it too. They burst into laughter. Kristy Meyer was practically doubled over.

"Pardon me," said Gorgo politely.

But Emily barely had time to register the apology or the laughter. Her attention was focused on the tiny ball of flame—like a little sun—that had come floating lazily out of the Stone as if expelled by the burp. It landed on the velvet bag in her other hand.

Which ignited and instantly became a mass of flame. Emily shrieked and hurled it away . . . right at the base of the stage curtains. And that's when things got really bad.

CHAPTER
FOUR

L et us step away from the proceedings for a moment. It's important.

Let us leave the school, and the Edelman household, and Earth, and even this universe, and travel to a dreadful, dark, dreary place.

In fact, to Dreadful Place, the cul-de-sac on the narrow, jagged peak that rose high above the intersection of Dark and Dreary (and overlooked Desolation Park, where the swing sets were known to be carnivorous).

On Dreadful Place stood—or squatted, really, in a sullen, threatening manner—a single dwelling, if you could call it that. The structure looked as though someone had found a particularly evil-minded architect and said, "I want you to combine the most sinister characteristics of a mansion with the baleful qualities of a fortified castle keep."

It was the sort of place that had at *least* one deep, deep dungeon where unspeakable acts were carried out, and a laboratory at the top of a high, high tower (only accessible via a mossy, crumbling spiral stone stairway) for equally unspeakable experiments. The sort of place where the decorative vegetation along the front pathway could kill you, or worse. The sort of place that was very definitely haunted, but where the ghosts were more afraid of the living inhabitants than vice versa.

And with good reason, because this home belonged to the Venomüch family.

Here's how you pronounce that unusual name: Start by saying the word "venomous." But when you get to the final syllable, imagine that you've just realized you have a spider in your mouth, so that the last part comes out as *"uuuch."*

And just as their uuuchy family name began with a V, so too do many of the words you might use to describe them: *Vile. Villainous. Vain. Vicious. Vengeful. Vindictive. Venal,* which is a fancy way of saying greedy. *Vituperative,* which is an even fancier way of saying bitter and nasty. And yes, *violent,* when it suited their wants and needs, and it usually did.

At this moment, Archduke Maligno Venomüch the

Thirteenth, proud patriarch of the Venomüch household, had a very specific want and need.

"I WANT and NEED that STONE!" he said, slamming a fist down onto the polished black marble tabletop, inadvertently squashing a roachlike bug the size of a mouse that had been trying to steal his dinner roll.

"Children!" snapped Archduchess Acrimina Deleteria Venomüch, Maligno's wife. "That's disgraceful!" The children, cursing under their breath, ceased jousting with their forks to skewer the flattened remains of the bug. Their mother immediately stabbed the bug herself and popped it into her mouth.

"Maaaaaaa!" said Maligna, their daughter.

"That's not fair," said Maligno the Fourteenth, their son. They were twins. Emily might say they were about her own age. That is, after she'd stopped screaming.

"SILENCE!" bellowed their father, bringing his fist down again. The children looked hopefully to see if there might be another squashed bug.

If Emily had indeed been observing the family, she would have seen four . . . well, let's not call them *people*. Let's call them *individuals*. They were seated around the black marble table, which was a repurposed gravestone.

The table was at the center of a shadowy room lined with dark wood and lit with sconces and candles. Crowding the walls were innumerable swords and other deadly weapons, as well as trophy plaques with heads of snarling grotesque beasts.

The Venomüches were dressed appropriately for the room. Emily would think of their clothes as old-fashioned formalwear from a time when people used muskets and fought duels and attended elaborate balls—although you certainly wouldn't want to attend any balls the Venomüch clan had been invited to. The clothes were all black. There were lots of ruffles and whatnot. Maligno the elder had a severe black beard and mustache. Acrimina was extremely beautiful without being the least bit attractive, the sort of beauty that you immediately knew hid an equally ugly soul.

The children were exactly the sort of offspring you would expect from such a couple.

Every member of the family had red eyes and very pointy teeth.

Looking at any of them, a person might think *Vampire.* But an actual vampire looking at them would think, *Help! Get me out of here!*

That's how scary the Venomüch family was.

"I want that Stone!" repeated Maligno Sr. "It has resurfaced. Someone has it. I can feel it! It's out there somewhere!"

"Yes, dear," said Acrimina absently. She was paging through an upscale housewares catalog featuring terrifying furniture and talking mirrors and assorted spooky chandeliers and the like.

"Dad," said Maligno Jr., "what's the big deal about that stupid Stone?"

"Yeah, Dad," said Maligna. "Who cares?"

From somewhere in the room came a growling noise.

"My darlings," said Maligno Sr., "I CARE!"

He smashed his fist on the gravestone table again. A crack appeared. Acrimina, without looking up, calmly dog-eared a page in the catalog featuring gravestone tabletops. There was another growl.

"But why?" said Maligna.

"Yeah, why?" echoed Maligno Jr.

"'Why?'" said Maligno Sr., his eyes flashing. "You know, for nearly limitless power to help us impose our will on the multiverse, work more evil, advance our family's perverse goals, et cetera, et cetera, et cetera."

"Oh, right, got it," said the children.

"And once the Stone is in our possession, we will be unstoppable! HA HA HA!"

The archduke didn't actually laugh. He didn't know how. That's how evil he was. He simply said, "Ha ha ha." The children, however, *were* able to laugh and did so, a sound like nails on a chalkboard, if the nails belonged to a yowling cat.

Once more the growl. The archduke's eyes flicked toward one of the mounted heads on the wall.

"I think that one's still alive, Dad," said Maligno Jr.

Acrimina, turning a page, said, "The Stone sounds lovely, dear. Very important."

"Yes, my love," said Maligno Sr.

"You should probably find a way to get it, don't you think?" said Acrimina.

"Yes, my love," repeated Maligno Sr. "But if the Stone has resurfaced, it must be in the possession of a Stonemaster."

"A Stonemaster," said Acrimina. "Yes, I suppose so."

The growl was continuing at a low, querulous pitch.

Without looking up from her catalog, Archduchess Acrimina Deleteria Venomüch flicked her wrist, sending her fountain pen streaking through the air so fast it was almost invisible. There was a sharp yelp. The growling ceased.

"I'm sure we can find some way to deal with the Stonemaster," said Acrimina.

At that moment—as much as you can say "at that moment," because time moves differently for different dimensions—the Stonemaster was riding in a minivan with her family, trying not to cry.

"Great job," said Hilary.

"Shut up," muttered Emily.

"It was awesome!" said Dougie.

"Shut up," said Hilary.

"*You* shut up!"

"All of you shut up!" said their dad from the front seat.

They were all soaking wet. They were not the only family in that condition. There were currently many cars filled with soaking-wet children and parents on their way home from the school. That's what happens when an automatic sprinkler system goes off in an auditorium.

It had been total chaos. After Emily shrieked and threw the burning bag, the flames jumped to the curtains and spread rapidly upward. The audience went from midlaugh to shouts of "Fire! FIRE!" as people screamed and rose out of their seats. Mr. Petersen had both hands clapped to the sides of his head. Emily was staring wide-eyed at the flames, repeating, "Oh, no. Oh, no." Then suddenly it was a tropical downpour as the sprinkler system came alive. Emily couldn't believe that so much water could come down so quickly.

Afterward, more chaos. Emily remembered the scene in snippets: The fire department arriving. Mr. Petersen saying, "I told you not to use fire!" Emily protesting that she hadn't. Emily's parents interrogating her in front of Mr. Petersen and the fire marshal, fingers pointing to the charred remains of the bag and the semi-melted cell phone inside.

"There are no matches or other incendiary device," said the fire marshal. "My guess is that the battery in that old cell phone somehow had a charge in it and shorted out, causing the fire. I've seen it happen before."

There was one other thing: In the midst of it all, Emily realized that the Stone was still glowing in her hand—*but no one else seemed to notice.* She was the only one who could see it. And she wished she couldn't. And as she thought that, the glow disappeared and the Stone was just a stone again.

"I can't believe this," said Hilary now from the back seat. "My new friends are already texting about it!"

"How did you get that phone!" said their mother to Hilary. "Give it to me!"

Hilary groaned and passed the device up to her.

"Honey," said Mrs. Edelman to Emily, "I just don't know what you were *thinking*. You're lucky they didn't expel you on the spot!"

"It wasn't my fault!" said Emily, but her mother wasn't paying attention because she was busy trying to pry her own shoe off. There was a suction-y *glorp*. "Ugh," said Mrs. Edelman, and she rolled down the window so she could dump the water out of her shoe.

Emily sat back in her seat, eyes welling up. Her mind was racing. What should she do? Tell her parents? Call her old friends back home? Call the police? Call the media? No, she couldn't tell anyone—who would believe her? She could prove everything by showing Gorgo to them, but what if they couldn't see him, just like they hadn't noticed the magic powers of the Stone? Or worse, what if Gorgo was lying about having to follow her commands and decided to hurt someone?

No. Emily would have to deal with this herself somehow. No one could know about the Stone and its power, ever.

. . . .

But someone *did* know about it. Or at least suspected something.

That someone was another student in Emily's grade. She had been sitting in the front row.

She was quiet, observant, serious. The sort of student of whom other students might say, *Oh, right, her. What was her name, again?*

Her name was Angela Rodriguez. She was, coincidentally, the person who had altered the yearbook descriptions of Kristy Meyer, but no one else knew that.

And while Angela might be the sort of person other people didn't notice or take an interest in, she noticed things and took an interest in them. Things like a deep voice emanating from the stone in Emily's hand, and a tiny spark that had appeared from nowhere and set everything ablaze.

Huh, Angela thought as she stood under the downpour from the sprinkler system. *That's interesting.*

The ground under Maligno Sr.'s boots made squelchy, rude noises as he made his way through the fetid swamp, his feet shrouded by the thick yellow vapor that hung low like a noxious blanket. Moonlight peeked through gnarled moss-covered branches overhead. Strange animals and insects added their eerie calls to the ominous digestive sounds of the swamp itself. Maligno, whistling cheerfully, paid them no heed.

He was carrying a large fireplace bellows propped on his shoulder. Every so often he would stop and sniff the air, adjust his course, and continue on his way.

In a clearing up ahead he spotted a lump rising out of the ground-hugging fog, like a small hillock. The smell he had been following—the smell of corruption and decay—grew much more intense.

"Perfect," he said.

He drew closer until he was standing over the form, the rotting remains of an animal the size of a large horse. It was not a pretty sight and smelled even worse than it looked.

Maligno circled the cadaver until it was between him and the moon, which hung a hand's width above the tree line. Then he crouched down and peered intently at the carcass—or more precisely, at the space directly above it, aligning his gaze with the moon. Maligno was motionless for several moments, straining to see, because what he was looking for was difficult to detect, even for someone with occult senses as keen as his.

There. Like a subtle, ghostly shadow passing between him and the moon. As he focused his attention on it he could see it better: a form like a giant, repulsive grub hovering over the dead animal, caressing it with innumerable tendrils and feelers as the spectral creature fed on its essence. A carrion shade.

"Hello, lovely," said Maligno.

Straightening up, he readied the bellows, holding the tip in the spot where he could still faintly see the carrion shade. Then he spread the handles, sucking the shade inside, and popped a small cork into the tip to plug the hole.

Maligno knew full well that the shade, being weightless and immaterial, could never retrieve the Stone. But he also knew that if directed by a very skilled practitioner of the very darkest arts—which Maligno most definitely was—the shade could *find* the Stone. And once the Stone was found, well, Maligno knew exactly what he'd send to *get* it. The thought made him smile cruelly.

Whistling contentedly, the bellows once again propped against his shoulder, Maligno started back home.

"Everything okay out there?" said Gorgo.

Emily was lying on her bed, fuming. After they had changed out of their wet clothes and the family had sat down for a late dinner, Hilary had said, "Hey, Dad, you guys better check the batteries in the smoke detectors. Who knows what Emily's going to get up to." So Emily had stormed upstairs to her room and slammed the door.

"Hello?" said Gorgo now, his voice emanating from the Stone.

Emily pulled the Stone out of her pocket, where she had automatically stuffed it during all the excitement.

"Be quiet, you," she said.

"What was all the shouting about?"

"Uh, let's see . . . maybe it was about you nearly burning down the school, and me getting blamed for it?"

"Goodness," he said. "Sorry about that."

"Oh, no, no, don't you worry about it at all," Emily said.

"No? Okay, great," Gorgo said. He seemed genuinely relieved.

"*Yes,* worry about it! You've ruined my life!"

"Listen, uh . . . what's your name?"

"What do you care?"

"I told you mine. If you want, I can just call you Master. Or Mistress. Or . . . Snack Food."

"It's *Emily*."

"Lovely name. A little short, but fine. Listen, Emily, I know what you're thinking," he said.

"I'm thinking, 'I'm sitting in my room, my life is ruined, I'm probably losing my mind, and I'm talking to a stone.'"

"Strictly speaking, you're talking to me. I just happen to be *in* the Stone."

"Well, guess what? Now I'm done," she said, and went to put the Stone in her sock drawer.

As she was burying it under her socks, Gorgo said, "Wait!"

"Gorgo, you have to obey me, right?" said Emily.

"Yes."

"Then stay in there and *don't talk to me!*" she said, and slammed the drawer shut.

Then she showered and brushed her teeth and got into bed and lay awake for a long time before finally falling asleep from sheer exhaustion.

And then woke with a gasp in the middle of the night, heart pounding, bathed in cold sweat, her mind filled with terror.

Because there was something in her room.

CHAPTER
FIVE

Emily lay as still as she could, not daring to move, barely daring to breathe.

There was something lurking in the darkness.

She couldn't hear it or see it, but she could *feel* it, the sheer foulness of its presence.

It wasn't Gorgo. She knew that. This was something else. Something far worse.

She was lying on her side. *It could be right behind me,* she thought, her skin crawling. *It could be right there, reaching for me.* But she felt paralyzed, unable to move a muscle, unable even to scream.

She could see, very dimly, her dresser across the room. Where her sock drawer was. The drawer she'd put the Stone in. The drawer she had slammed shut.

The drawer was open.

At that moment the clouds parted and a shaft of moonlight drew a distorted silvery rectangle on the dresser and the wall. And she saw it.

Something made of smoke and shadow and horror. Somehow transparent and immaterial, yet there all the same, a blob covered with hideous feelers and antennae that were blindly waving about, some of them now tracing the contours of the dresser. Searching.

The feelers continued to wander insidiously over the surface of the dresser, more and more of them joining in. Then the writhing shadow suddenly froze, quivering with apparent excitement. Emily felt a burst of nausea and vertigo. It had found the Stone. It was touching it. And the room spun and it seemed she was falling into an abyss and she felt she would go mad from fear and then she heard her own voice say, *"Awaken!"*

The light was blinding, pure, a thousand suns radiating forth from her drawer, the shadow blown away like mist before a gale. In that moment Emily heard a harsh, inhuman screech that she was certain would wake the entire neighborhood.

She turned on the light and leaped from her bed, ran to slam the drawer shut, then ran out of her room, pulling the door shut behind her before sprinting to her parents' room.

She paused, her hand on the doorknob. She could hear her dad snoring through the closed door. She padded down the hall and checked on Dougie and Hilary. They were both still asleep.

If she said she'd had a bad dream, her parents would scold her for waking them and send her back to her room. If she told them the truth, they'd think she was crazy.

She went downstairs, turned on the living room light, and sat in a chair, shivering. She was still sitting there, eyes wide open, when the sun came up.

I have to get rid of the Stone, thought Emily. *I have to.* Exhausted, halfway through a day that seemed nearly as nightmarish as the night before had been, she was trudging through the school halls toward her locker, eyes fixed on the floor.

Until yesterday, she had just been the Weird New Girl Who Somehow Had Something Wrong with Her. As of this morning, owing to all the fun at the talent show, she had become the Weird New Girl Who Had Gotten Up On Stage, Panicked, Belched Hugely, Then Tried to Burn Down the School.

If she had been at zero on the social scale before, she was now somewhere deep, deep, deep in the negative range.

All day it had been the same, no matter what classroom Emily was in or where she was in the halls: stares, whispers, pointing fingers, snickering. And burps. Lots and lots of burps. Boys burping on cue as she walked past, then barely smothering giggles. *How is it that all boys know how to burp like that?* she wondered. *Are there secret lessons?*

Even the teachers looked at her funnily—the worried, guarded expression teachers wore when they had a particularly troubled and troublesome student in their class. There was a trio of teachers up ahead of her now in the corridor, two women and a man. As soon as they saw Emily, their conversation ceased, and their eyes followed her as she approached and then passed them. When she glanced back from the end of the hallway, they were huddled even closer in an animated conspiratorial conversation. The male teacher spotted her observing them and quickly hushed the others.

It wasn't me! Emily wanted to scream. *It was a demon trapped in this magic Stone I found!*

Which, she knew, would have the same effect as trying to drown a fire with a big bucket of gasoline. And she didn't expect any sympathy if she were to describe the hideous spirit that had appeared in her room last night. She trudged on.

She was not wearing socks. In the morning she had eaten her breakfast in silence while Dougie chattered away and kicked at her legs under the table. After eating, Emily had darted into her room, holding her breath as she grabbed a change of clothes from her dresser. She couldn't make herself open her sock drawer.

Meaning she had left the Stone in the drawer when she went to school. Which turned out to be one of the most difficult things she had ever done. As if the Stone was calling out to her, whimpering, desperate to go with her. It felt completely wrong to leave it there, as though she were abandoning a puppy alongside a desolate stretch of highway. That, or like a scene in a zombie movie where the hero puts her weapon down for juuuuust a moment so she can take a quick refreshing dip in a lake, and you scream, *Don't do that! Don't do that!*

But Emily still couldn't even think of touching the Stone, let alone taking it with her.

She felt it calling to her the whole time she was walking to school. Walking to Clearview School was a strategy she had decided on this morning. A quick glance at a map had proved that she could do it in about half an hour, thereby avoiding the environment most toxic and dangerous for the outcast: the school bus. So she walked Dougie to the bus stop and then went her own way.

The town of Clearview was a peaceful, pleasant place, the houses and lawns modest and neatly maintained. But today it felt like enemy territory. The whole way Emily felt as if she was being observed, as if people were snickering at her from their windows as she walked by. The feeling got worse when a dark-haired girl emerged from a house, silently watched her pass, and then started following her. Not just walking behind her: the mysterious girl had seemed intent on catching up to Emily. Emily accelerated.

And then she had arrived at school and been barraged with burps and stares and whispers and hushed giggles.

She was nearing her locker now. An image of last night's terrifying specter flashed in her mind for the hundredth time, and she tried to block it out. It was the Stone, she knew. The Stone was the problem. *She had to get rid of it.*

Her locker was close enough to the auditorium that she could see the yellow DO NOT ENTER tape stretching across the doorway and hear the midpitched hum of the blowers the work crew had put in there to try to dry everything out.

"I have to get rid of the Stone," she said aloud.

"What's that? Is everything okay, Emily?"

The voice was sugary, cloying, mocking in its false concern. A bowl of honey-covered wasps.

Emily paused, her locker halfway open, and mentally steeled herself for whatever was about to happen.

"What do you want, Kristy," she said, keeping her gaze fixed on the depths of her locker. She didn't have to look to know Kristy was right there, her henchmen—hench*girls*—arrayed behind her, grinning in anticipation.

"Well," said Kristy, "I just wanted to say you did a *great* job last night. You were *on fire!* Ha ha ha ha!!!"

Kristy and her friends all went stumbling away, too weak with laughter and self-congratulation to walk properly. Grimly shoving books into her locker and taking other ones out, Emily muttered, "That's not even a good joke. It's not even *funny*."

"No, it isn't," said another voice.

This time Emily turned.

It was the dark-haired girl, the mysterious one from this morning. The one who had followed her.

"Hi. My name is Angela," said the girl. "Angela Rodriguez."

She stuck out her hand. Emily looked at it. Then she noticed the clusters of other kids lingering casually in the vicinity, hoping for more entertainment. She was aware of a sudden vacuum, the non-sound that results when kids are trying to eavesdrop on a conversation without appearing to do so.

"Can we talk?" Angela said quietly.

Emily looked at Angela's serious expression. Then she looked at the other kids, noting the sly glances, smirks, furtive murmuring. Everyone was waiting to see what happened next.

In that moment, Emily rapidly performed the sort of complex social calculation that kids are very good at. It went like this: either (a) this Angela was another mean girl like Kristy, and this apparently friendly overture was actually some sort of twisted, cruel ploy; or (b) Angela was an outcast like Emily.

If you've ever been an outcast—which, if you're an interesting person, you probably have—you will understand the following paradox: often the very *last* thing you want when you're an outcast is the pity or attention of *another* outcast.

And so Emily looked at the hand outstretched in friendship and mistakenly saw nothing but danger.

Angela finally dropped her hand. "I want to talk to you," she said.

"Well, *I* don't want to talk to *you*," said Emily, and slammed her locker shut and stalked off.

At dinner, Hilary said, "Here's a burned piece, Emily. You might like it."

"Hey, why don't you burp again?" added Dougie. "BUURRRRP!"

"Dougie!" said their mom, but Emily noticed that both she and their father were fighting to stifle their own laughter.

After dinner Emily sat at the kitchen table, trying to do her homework. Normally she'd do it in her room, but she didn't want to go in there, knowing that the Stone — and Gorgo — were waiting for her in her sock drawer.

It was hard to concentrate.

Partially because of the tortured honking and squawking noises that indicated her father was practicing his saxophone.

Partially because of the throbbing in her toe, which she had stubbed when she had knocked over her father's music stand, which had happened when she was chasing Dougie, which she had done because he kept appearing in the doorway to zing her with rubber bands. And of course *she* was the one who got yelled at.

Partially because Emily could overhear her sister now on the phone with her friends: "I *know!* Totally, like, nearly *burned it down.* I am. So. Embarrassed. To be her sister."

And partially because her mom kept interrupting her, coming into the room with a tablet computer and saying things such as "Ooh, look at this! Look at the lovely dress she'll be wearing!" and "Ooh! Emily, don't you want to see where they're holding the wedding?"

The wedding. Some cousin. All Emily knew was that the ceremony was tomorrow and it would be several hours of driving to get there.

So those things all made it hard to concentrate. But mostly it was hard because every math problem in front of Emily seemed to go something like, "If Avery needs to buy apples and flour but has only $12, *how will she ever get rid of the magic Stone she found that has a demon in it that wants to eat her?*"

Instead of math answers, Emily kept scribbling and crossing out things:

~~Leave Stone in park?~~
~~Throw away?~~
~~Break with hammer?~~
~~Bury?~~
Flush down toilet?

None of that would work, she thought.

"Emily, look at this!"

Her mom again, standing at the table, holding the tablet computer. She must have come in without Emily even noticing.

"Mom, I'm trying to do my homework."

"But look how nice the venue for the reception is!"

She turned the screen so Emily could see it. "See? It's called the Overlook Bay Resort. Doesn't it look—hey!"

Emily had snatched the tablet out of her mother's hands and was staring fixedly at the image on the screen: an aerial shot of some sort of fancy resort perched near the edge of a high cliff, a cliff that overlooked a large bay.

"Well, you certainly seem interested now," said her mother.

"What's that?" said Emily, pointing.

"That's water, sweetie. What did you think it was?"

"I mean, is it a lake?"

"It's a bay. Like the name of the resort says."

"A bay that connects to the ocean?"

"Yes — why?"

"Nothing," said Emily, and handed the tablet back to her.

"Are you all right? You look flushed."

"I'm fine. I'm a lot better now."

When her mom left the room, Emily wrote, THROW STONE BACK INTO OCEAN WHERE IT CAME FROM and circled it three times.

She stayed up until her parents ordered her to bed. Then she showered and brushed her teeth, took a deep breath, and went into her room.

She closed the door behind her and leaned against it, regarding the sock drawer as if it were her enemy. Then, keeping as far away from it as possible, Emily made her way to her bed and climbed in. She kept the light on. She had decided that she wasn't going to sleep: she'd stay up all night again and then sleep on the car trip the next day. Even so, her eyelids began to droop, then closed altogether as she drifted off.

"Doot doot doooo . . ."

She opened her eyes.

"La la la laaa . . ."

It was Gorgo's muffled voice, coming from the drawer as he crooned tunelessly to himself.

"Hmm hmm hmm hmm doot doooo . . ."

Well, not exactly "to himself." The sort of humming you do with an innocent air in an attempt to get someone to pay attention to you and respond. Emily didn't.

"Shoobie doo waaa . . ."

She stared fixedly at the moon shining through the window. There was a longer silence. Gorgo must have given up. Phew. Her eyes started to close again.

"Doop doobity doo waa waaaaaa . . ."

Emily snapped her eyes open, threw back the covers, stomped over to the dresser, and jerked open the sock drawer.

"Would you be quiet!" she hissed.

"Okay," said a voice from somewhere underneath the socks. "But since you posed that as a question, I'm taking it to mean that I'm now allowed to talk to you and will quickly take this opportunity to say that I *reee-allly* think we should chat!"

"No!" she said.

He was silent.

"Okay, why?" she said.

"First of all, can I come out? It's very uncomfortable in here like this. My leg is asleep."

Emily thought about it.

"You have to be quiet. And no fires!"

"Of course."

She fished around under the socks until she found the Stone, then held it up. Again, without knowing exactly why, she said, "Awaken."

The Stone awoke, the gentle glow returning. Emily had seen it happen before, but still she couldn't help gasping.

She twisted the Stone this way and that. Again she had the illusion of looking through a small window, the tiny icons floating gently as if suspended in an infinite space. The moon rotating in the upper right-hand corner seemed to have waned just the slightest amount.

"No rush or anything, but I seriously can't even feel my foot now," said Gorgo.

"Sorry. How do I do it, again?"

"You know the word."

"What? Oh, right. Um . . . *abrakadonkulous*."

This time there was no explosion. Instead, Gorgo reversed his folding routine: A small cube popped out of the Stone and landed on the floor next to Emily. Then, in a series of rapid movements, it unfolded and inflated its way into being Gorgo.

"Ah, that's so much better!" he said, even though his head was brushing the ceiling. He began vigorously massaging one of his legs. "Ugh. Don't you hate it when your foot goes all numb, and then it's the pins and needles, and—"

"Gorgo, what is going on?"

"Huh?"

"There was . . . *something* in my room last night."

"Ah, right. I thought I felt something. Some sort of shade or spirit, probably sniffing around after the Stone."

"Why?"

He shrugged. "Dunno. Maybe someone sent it. Or maybe it just showed up, drawn by the Stone," he said. "You're about to say 'why' again, aren't you."

"Yes. *Why.* Why would that thing be drawn to this Stone?"

"Because it's a *Stone.* They're incredibly powerful, Stones are. Powerful and rare. A Stonemaster can use them to work great magics. That's a very ancient relic you have there. Well, sort of *modern* ancient. The first Stones were massive. You've heard of Stonehenge, right?

Well, those are really old-fashioned. You couldn't move them anywhere. The one you have, though, it's portable, or, uh . . ."

"Mobile?" said Emily.

"Right!"

"A mobile . . . Stone?"

"Precisely!"

"A mobile Stone for casting spells."

"Right again."

"It's a Mobile. Spell. Stone."

"You seem fixated on that."

"It's like a mobile cell phone."

"Not sure what you're talking about, but if you say so."

"What are all these thingies floating around?" Emily swiped at the icons experimentally, just like you would do with a touchscreen device. And sure enough, her motion caused those icons to disappear offscreen, replaced by new ones that floated in from the side. "They look like apps," she said.

"So you *do* know something," said Gorgo. "Except it's pronounced 'apths.'"

"Apps?"

"No, *apths*. With a *th* sound."

"What's an 'apth'?"

"It stands for 'applied process thaumaturgical.' They're like little spells."

"Thauma . . ."

"Thaumaturgy. Magic. I think there's an apth for pretty much anything you want to do. But you have to be *very careful* with them. But hey, you're the Stonemaster."

"No, I'm not," said Emily. "I'm just a normal kid. Why is this happening to me?"

He shrugged. "Who knows. Some prophecy or whatever. Are you the seventh son of a seventh son?"

"What? No. I'm not anyone's son."

"How is that possible?"

"Because I'm a girl?"

"Right! Of course! Okay—seventh daughter of a seventh daughter?"

"No."

"Seventh daughter of a seventh son?"

"No."

"Seventh male *or* female offspring of *any* possible combination of—"

"I can't be the seventh *anything*. I only have a brother and a sister!"

"Ah. So, lemme see. There's you, your brother, your sister . . ." said Gorgo, counting off on his talons. "That's, uh . . ."

"Three," said Emily, narrowing her eyes.

"Of course it is. And three is . . . ?"

"Less than seven."

"Are you certain?"

"Fairly certain, yes," said Emily.

"Huh," said Gorgo, scratching his chin in perplexity. "So the seventh-offspring-of-seventh-offspring thing wouldn't explain it. Aha! How about third cousin twice removed of twin great nephews of a descendent of the fourth high king of GlackenKlack who reigned during—" He paused. "I'm guessing from your expression that you don't know what GlackenKlack is."

"I don't even know what a third cousin twice removed is."

"Neither do I, really. Who does? Look, sometimes these things just *happen*. You got the Stone because you deserve it for some reason. I imagine you're plucky and adventurous and full of derring-do."

Emily thought about that.

"I'm not *any* of those things. Especially the adventurous part. I hate adventures."

"I think you'd better start developing a taste for them."

"If something magical is going to happen, why can't it be something normal? Like, a coin that you have to wish twice on, or . . . or finding out that I'm supposed to go to a boarding school for wizards or something?"

"Boarding school for wizards? Ha ha ha! That's ridiculous. Absurd. Hee hee hee!"

"And what about you?" she said. "Do all Stones have a demon trapped inside them?"

"Okay, first, not a demon, and second, no. I think it was just a useful vessel for the person who trapped me in there."

"And why did they?"

"I'd rather not tell you."

"But you'd have to if I commanded you to."

"Yes. But . . . I think maybe you don't want to know."

He looked at her evenly. She shuddered.

"Okay," she said. She was noting now that in addition to the bumps and spikes on his gray-green skin, he had an impressive assortment of scars. She decided she didn't want to know where those came from, either. Another thing she noticed: "Where're all the flames?"

"Eh." Gorgo shrugged. "That's mostly for show. I can control them, unless I get excited or angry. Or nervous."

"Or burp."

"I really am sorry about that."

"Emily, are you talking to someone?"

It was her mother, outside her door.

"Quick!" said Emily. Gorgo sighed but folded himself up and disappeared into the Stone.

"Emily," said her mother, opening the door. "What are you doing out of bed? Get to sleep! We've got a long drive tomorrow!"

Before Emily got into bed, she went to put the Stone into her drawer again.

"Hey, c'mon," said Gorgo. "I get so bored in here."

"Gorgo?" she said.

"Yes?"

"Can you please leave me alone? While you're in there, I want you to plug your ears and close your eyes and stop paying attention to me and stop talking to me."

"Yes, Stonemaster."

"I'm not a Stonemaster!"

"Yes, Mistress Snack Food."

"And don't call me that!"

"Yes, Mistress."

"Okay," she said, and started to put the Stone into the drawer again.

"But one last thing," said Gorgo. "And I'm not just saying this because I'm bound to serve you for eternity until such time as I can somehow free myself and devour you. Which, believe me, I will. I don't know anything about how to use that Stone. But I do know this:

That thing that showed up last night? That was nothing. Sooner or later other things will show up. Worse things, things that you can't drive off or destroy with a bit of light."

"Fine," said Emily.

"And Emily," said Gorgo, "you can't just get rid of the Stone. I know you want to, but you're stuck with it."

We'll see about that, thought Emily, and shut the drawer.

CHAPTER
SIX

Maligno Venomüch Sr. walked along a dark, stone-lined hallway. The only illumination came from a flaming torch in his hand. *Things* skittered out of the way as he approached. In his other hand he was holding the raw, bloody haunch of some sort of animal.

He came to a thick wooden door.

There was a deep snarl from the other side.

"Hello, dogg," he said. The second *g* was audible. The word sounded like "daw-guh-guh."

There was more snarling.

"I have a present for you."

Maligno unlatched a smaller door within the door and pushed the haunch through. It was immediately yanked out of his hand. There was more snarling, and ripping and tearing and chewing and swallowing noises. Then,

"Ptoooey." The thigh bone from the haunch sailed out of the smaller door and hit the opposite wall before falling to the moist stones below. It had been picked clean.

Maligno had something else in his hand: a small jar containing a writhing patch of darkness, a tiny remnant of the carrion shade he had sent to find the Stone. He opened the jar, stuck it through the smaller door, and felt the dogg sniffing at it.

"Good dogg," said Maligno. "Now *fetch*."

The drive to the wedding was long. Emily slept a lot. She had finally fallen asleep the night before despite herself, but she still felt as if she could sleep for three days straight.

Her sister sat in the third row of the minivan and listened to music, occasionally singing out loud in her off-key voice. Dougie sat next to Emily in the second row, sometimes poking her in the ribs to wake her up, and once dipping his finger into his yogurt shake and then sticking his finger into her ear, until she screamed at him and her parents scolded her and ordered her into the back row with Hilary. Then she stared out the window and worked on her plan to get rid of the Stone.

. . . .

The wedding was lovely. Her cousin was beautiful in her dress. The groom was, well, well-groomed and handsome. Grownups cried and blew their noses like trumpets. Emily's mother sobbed.

Emily, her thoughts dominated by how to get rid of the Stone, barely registered any of it.

Afterward, as they drove to the reception at the fancy resort on the high bluff above the bay, Emily's mother said, "Wasn't it *lovely*?"

"What?" said Emily. "Uh, yes. Lovely."

Meanwhile, a dogg was sniffing and snuffling its way through many dimensions, following a particular trail of magic. A path of spirit slime, left by Emily's nocturnal visitor.

Portals opened before and closed after the animal, like someone unzipping and then zipping a dogg-size portion of reality, allowing it to move from world to world, universe to universe. Its sudden appearance— and its fearful *physical* appearance—was generally greeted with screams of terror in each location as it passed through: an office building where the work- ers looked like furniture and the furniture looked like people; an island filled with purple cloud creatures; a snow-covered realm where an insufferable talking lion was pontificating to a group of children, pausing in his lecture to yelp in surprise when the dogg materialized and just as quickly vanished.

With each world, the dogg was getting closer to the Stone.

The wedding reception was held on a flagstone courtyard in the back of the resort. There were white tablecloths on the tables and an extensive buffet, the evening tableau illuminated by dozens of glowing paper lanterns. Hilary flirted with the waiters. Dougie used his spoon to catapult peas at other tables. Emily ate her food without tasting it, interacting with her family only enough to prevent Dougie from sticking a buttered muffin onto her forearm.

As soon as the wedding band started up and the guests headed to the dance floor, Emily made her move.

There was a broad lawn beyond the courtyard. It led to the cliff above the bay. Wooded areas flanked the lawn on both sides. Making sure no one saw her, Emily slipped off the flagstone and onto the lawn, and then to the trees. She followed a path that she figured would take her parallel to the shoreline, peering up through the branches at the moon now and then to make sure she maintained her course.

She went deeper into the woods, the music fading behind her. When she could no longer hear the band at all, she turned left and headed toward where she thought the cliff edge and the water would be. Sure enough, after a short while the trees thinned out and then stopped altogether, and there was a band of rocky ground between the woods and the edge of the cliff.

When she got a few feet from the edge, she slowed and then cautiously inched forward. Emily had never been a huge fan of dresses, so after much debate with her mother that morning, she had been allowed to wear a pair of nice pants with a fancy embroidered top to the wedding. Now she was wishing she were wearing shorts, because she would have preferred to crawl the remaining distance to the edge.

"I. Hate. Heights," she muttered to no one, taking the few shaky steps she needed to get all the way to the lip.

She peeked over the edge and instantly regretted it, her head swimming. Far below her was a thin strip of rocky beach and then the calm waters of the bay. She quickly scrambled back from the precipice and caught her breath.

"*Hate* them."

She opened her little beaded purse and pulled out the Stone.

"Goodbye," she said. "And good riddance!"

Then, drawing back her arm, Emily hurled the Stone with all her might toward the bay. She watched it fly in a high arc, following its path until it landed in the water with a faint splash.

"There," she said. "That's done!"

Then she turned to walk away.

Phew. That was over. Now she could go back to being a normal kid who—

What was that sound? Like another splash, but a splash in *reverse,* as if something had been ejected forcefully from the water. Emily spun around and—

"WHOA!"

She flinched, turning her head away and closing her eyes, and jerked her hands up reflexively to ward off the object that was streaking directly at her—just in time to catch it in her right hand, her fingers curling around it automatically. Her face still turned away and scrunched in a grimace, she waited for the sting of the impact to reach her brain. It never arrived. She opened her eyes and looked at the object in her hand.

It was the Stone.

"No," she said. "I can*not* be*lieve* this."

The Stone had come tumbling back at her at the same speed she had thrown it—faster, even—but instead of painfully slapping into her hand like a hard-thrown baseball, it had slowed at the very last moment and nestled itself perfectly into her waiting palm.

"No!" said Emily. "Get out of here!" And she hurled the Stone away again.

This time it got as far as a few feet above the water before coming to an abrupt, quivering halt, then reversed direction again to fly right back to Emily's hand.

"Argh!"

She threw the Stone again. It didn't even travel halfway to the water.

"No!"

Again. Back it came. Again. Right back to her hand.

"NO!" Again, again, and again she threw it, each time the Stone reversing course after shorter and shorter intervals, until Emily was throwing it and it was zooming back to her hand like a child's paddle ball game.

"Stop it!" she said. "Get away from me!" She looked around desperately. *There.* A big rock. She ran over to it, used all her might to tilt it enough so that there was a space underneath, wedged the Stone into the space, and lowered the rock. Then she found other rocks and piled them atop and around the first rock until there was a sizable mound.

"Stay there!" she said, and started to back away. "Stay. Stay!" She backed away a few more steps. Nothing. Then a few more steps. Nothing. A few more.

Nothing. The Stone was trapped under the other rocks, hopefully forever.

"Yesssss." Emily wiped her brow, turned, and started to walk toward the trees.

There was a scraping, grinding noise. A stone-on-stone sound, the sort a magic Stone might make if it was trying to wiggle itself out from under a much larger, heavier stone that was itself weighed down by other stones.

Emily stopped. The scraping stopped. She took another step. Another scrape. She took three more steps. More scraping, and then the distinct sound of a few of the smaller stones rolling off the pile.

Emily broke into a run. Behind her was the sound of a mound of rocks collapsing.

Anyone observing the scene for the next minute or so would have witnessed something very odd: a young girl running in panicked circles and zigzags and dodging behind trees, shouting, "No! Go away! Keep away from me!" as if she were playing a game of tag in a forest with invisible opponents. A sharp-eyed observer would have noted that she was indeed being pursued, and tenaciously so, by what appeared to be a levitating stone.

Emily wove through the trees, panting. She was exhausted but sensed that she was opening a bit of a lead on the Stone, and that gave her more strength. She glanced over her shoulder now as she ran, didn't see the Stone, and then—*ooof!* A root caught her foot and sent her sprawling face first onto the leafy forest ground. She raised herself up on her hands and—

"EEEIIEEE!!!"

Directly in front of her, not three feet away, crouched *something.*

It looked to Emily like the largest, most ferocious dog she had ever seen, its muscular body the size of a lion, its open, slavering jaws impossibly large and tooth filled, its paws equipped with talons as long as steak knives. And its eyes: green glowing eyes, eyes burning with a bloodthirsty animal intelligence.

Eyes focused on her.

With a savage, hideous snarl, the creature leaped.

Emily threw herself down again, covering her head. She felt the rush of wind as the creature passed directly over her. Then she heard a crunch, followed by the sound of four viciously clawed paws returning to the earth, and then the sound of those paws galloping away from her.

She flipped over and propped herself up on her elbows. The creature was indeed fleeing from her. It was running away, the Stone was nowhere to be seen, and she was safe. That thing must have taken the Stone! She was free!

"I did it," she said. "I *did* it!"

Then she felt the tugging.

As though every cell in her body was being tugged in the direction of the beast, and in the space of about a second the tugging went from *Hmmm, what's that* to *Wow, that's insistent* to *Wait! Help! Now I'm being dragged through the woods toward that fleeing monster dog creature!*

Because that's exactly what was happening. Whatever connection Emily had had with the Stone, it was still there, and instead of the Stone following *her, she* was now following the Stone. Which, unfortunately, was in the slavering many-toothed jaws of a very powerful dogg. That crunch she'd heard, she realized now, had been the sound of the creature snapping the Stone out of the air, much like a normal dog snagging a Frisbee.

Emily was starting to accelerate, tumbling and

rolling and then sliding headfirst over the leafy ground. She grabbed at trees and roots in an attempt to slow herself down, but it was no use. "Help!" she screamed. "Help!"

Where was she going? Where was that terrifying doglike creature dragging her?

A moment later she could hear music and the trees vanished and she was being dragged across the giant lawn between the edge of the cliff and the courtyard where people were dancing, oblivious to her plight.

"HEEEEEEEeeeeeeeeelp!" she yelled as she zoomed past.

On the dance floor, Emily's parents were cha-chaing enthusiastically. They twirled around and her mother was momentarily facing out toward the lawn, and then they spun again.

Over the music her mother said, "Does someone here have a dog?"

"A what?"

"A dog. A big dog."

"Dunno. Why?"

"I thought I saw something."

She shrugged and they kept dancing.

When the creature reached the woods on the other

side of the lawn, it ran complicated loops around several trees and then went running back the direction it had come from. And Emily, hollering and scrabbling at the ground, was pulled along with it, as though they were connected by a giant rubber band.

"HEEEEEeeeeeeeelp!" she yelled again as she was once more dragged across the lawn, now in the opposite direction.

Emily's parents came out of another spin and her father dipped her mother. Mrs. Edelman leaned her head back gracefully, giving her an upside-down view of the lawn. Her eyebrows rose — or lowered, in this case, because the top of her head was pointing to the ground.

When Mr. Edelman pulled Mrs. Edelman up again, she said, "Are you *sure* no one has a dog here? That Emily might be playing with?"

"I don't know. Why do you keep asking?"

"Never mind."

"Okay."

Emily was zooming through the woods again, the music dropping away. The creature seemed tireless, as if it could pull her forever. Where was it going? Was it going to run around the whole planet? They changed direction again and were out of the trees once more — and the creature was running straight toward the cliff's edge.

"Wait! No!"

In that instant Emily saw, hovering a few feet beyond the edge of the cliff, what looked like some sort of portal — as if someone had unzipped part of the world, distorting it and revealing a pitch-black nothingness beyond, rimmed by crackling light. The creature was racing directly toward the portal, and right then Emily understood its plan — it was going to leap off the cliff and through the portal, and whether she got pulled along with it or stayed on this side, the outcome didn't seem promising. As she was realizing that, the beast made its leap.

"No!" Emily screamed, grabbing at and just managing to snag a root with one hand.

The animal reacted like a standard dog would if it leaped forward and suddenly came to the end of its chain: it was jerked violently backwards, its bottom half swinging like a pendulum, and then the creature started to fall.

The initial shock caused Emily to cry out, nearly wrenching the root from her grasp, but she held fast.

Then, fleetingly, the sensation of tugging vanished.

But Emily didn't celebrate. Instead she whispered, "Oh, no." Then she quickly grabbed the root with her other hand as well.

Because she knew exactly what this was: It was the moment when a mountain climber slipped and went into free fall. And her partner, tethered to her by a rope, had better get a very good grip on the mountain *right now,* because in half a heartbeat the plummeting partner was going to reach the end of the rope and—

"*Arrrgh!*"

It felt as though Emily's shoulders were going to pop out of their sockets. She could hear a growl rising up from somewhere down the cliff face. The weight pulling at her was terrible, enormous, and now her fingers were slipping, slipping; she couldn't hold on to the root any longer, couldn't even scream if she wanted to, and then a final desperate notion came to her.

"Abra . . ." she gasped, "ka . . . *donkulous!*"

There was a strange unfolding noise, and a yelp, and Gorgo's voice saying, "What the . . . ?!"

And then Emily had a split second for one final realization: That she'd just made a fatal mistake. Because now she wasn't holding just the creature's weight. She was holding Gorgo's, too.

Then her fingers lost their grip and she slid feet first toward the cliff, clawing uselessly at the dirt, and then she went screaming helplessly over the edge. And kept screaming the whole way down.

CHAPTER
SEVEN

EEEEEEEEEEEEEEEEEEEEEEEEOOOF!"

Emily lay stunned, looking up at several hundred feet of cliff face and the night sky beyond.

Then Gorgo's face blocked her view.

"Oh, for Blarg's sake," he said. "This is ridiculous."

"Wha—?" wheezed Emily. "Am I dead?"

"Unfortunately, no," said Gorgo.

"You . . . caught . . . me," managed Emily with some effort. She was afraid to move, fearing that every single bone in her body was broken. *Had* to be broken.

"Yes, I caught you." He seemed exasperated. A few jets of flame erupted briefly from his scalp.

"You saved my life," said Emily.

"Don't rub it in!" said Gorgo. "It was a reflex! Totally

91

automatic! You summon me, suddenly I'm in free fall and I grab at this dogg, and right when I land, something nearly lands on my head and I just reach and grab it, and fantastic, great, it turns out to be you."

"Thank . . . you."

"Argh. Had I known, I wouldn't have bothered, and then I'd be free. And having dinner. Hey, would you leggo?"

Emily wasn't sure to whom this last part was directed, but she did hear growling.

"Here, stand up," said Gorgo, and he placed Emily on her feet. To her surprise she didn't topple over, and apart from a collection of scrapes and bruises she was apparently uninjured.

She and Gorgo were standing on the rocky shore at the base of the cliff. Gorgo had his hands on his hips, observing with a frown the creature clamped onto his left ankle and shaking its head back and forth as if it was trying to rip Gorgo to pieces.

"What," said Emily, "is *that?*"

"That," said Gorgo, "is a dogg."

"A daw-guh-guh-guh?"

"Guh-*guh*. Two 'guhs.' A daw-guh-guh-*guh*, with three 'guhs,' is an entirely different type of creature, something very scary."

"*This* is *not* very scary?" said Emily, feeling a bit dizzy and disoriented after being roughly dragged back and forth through a forest and then falling from a height that should have left her in pancake form.

"Scary? I always thought doggs were kind of cute," said Gorgo. "Good daw-guh-guh-y." He patted it on the head. The dogg took the opportunity to release Gorgo's ankle and clamp its jaws around his forearm instead. Green slobber glowed on Gorgo's leg where the dogg had been attached, but otherwise Gorgo seemed unharmed.

"Adorable," said Gorgo. "So what in the twenty-seven levels of darkness were you doing? Did you somehow summon this dogg to play fetch?"

"Summon it? I tried to throw away the Stone, and then I couldn't, and the Stone kept chasing me, and then the *dogg* appeared, and it grabbed the Stone, and—"

"Aha. Someone sent the dogg for the Stone. How interesting."

"Is it?"

"First off, didn't I tell you that you couldn't get rid of the Stone? It's yours. You are its. You're a Stonemaster. You're tied together. Second, this dogg didn't just show up on its own. They don't do that. There's someone out there who wants this Stone and sent the dogg after it. Ah—of course!"

"What?"

"That shade that appeared in your room—that was just to find the Stone and lay a trail. It's easy to send a weightless spirit. Sending something flesh and blood, that requires real effort. It's lucky they just sent a dogg. If they'd sent a doggg, you'd be in trouble. Although a doggg probably would have just eaten you and botched the job."

"I saw something up there, like a hole in the world." Emily looked up, but the pitch-black nothingness wasn't there anymore.

"Sure. Whoever wants the Stone opened up a portal of some kind. I'm sure it's closed now. Those things are difficult to manage." Gorgo looked at the dogg, who was still hanging from his arm. "Who's a good boy! Who's a cutie!" The dogg growled in response and made more tearing motions with its head.

"Now what?" said Emily.

"Well, I doubt that whoever sent this guy can open the portal again. He's stuck here. Do you want a pet?"

"*That?!*"

"What's the problem? It's just a dogg, not a doggg."

"Get rid of it!"

"Get rid of it?" repeated Gorgo. "All right," he said reluctantly, and raised his other fist.

"Wait!" said Emily. "What are you going to do?"

"You said to get rid of it."

"I didn't mean . . . you know."

"You asked me to get rid of it, and that's the way I'd get rid of it. If you don't like that, why don't *you* get rid of it? You've got the Stone."

The Stone! Where was it?

Emily looked around the beach, turning left and right. The Stone was nowhere to be seen.

"Ahem," said Gorgo, and inclined his head toward her beaded purse, which was somehow still over her shoulder.

She felt the purse — and yes, there it was. The Stone had found its own way in there without her even noticing. Removing it from the purse, Emily held up the Stone and touched the surface with her other hand.

"Awaken."

Sure enough, the familiar glow returned, illuminating her face.

"What should I do?" she said.

"Dunno. You're the Stonemaster."

"No, I'm not."

"Whatever. Figure it out. Maybe there's some sort of portal apth in there, something that will let you send the dogg back."

Emily examined the dancing runes and icons. Nothing called out to her.

"I don't know."

"Keep looking."

She swiped, swiped, and swiped some more. The dogg continued to worry at Gorgo's forearm. "Goo'boy. Suuuuch a goo'boy," said Gorgo, patting its head. The dogg let go and switched arms.

Emily swiped again. The dancing icons seemed endless. *How about this?* She jabbed at one that seemed to call out to her. There was a sound like the muffled popping of thousands of kernels of popcorn.

"Huh. Well, I imagine it's at least vanished from view," said Gorgo.

His voice was coming from within a dense and Gorgo-shaped arrangement of flowers, his entire body now covered by a two-foot-thick layer of blossoms. The dogg, still squirming, was similarly concealed.

"Dang it!" said Emily, and tapped the apth again to shut it off. The flower petals fell to the ground in a heap, revealing Gorgo and the dogg once again.

"Something else?" suggested Gorgo.

"I'm trying," said Emily, tapping on another apth.

"Would you quit playing around?" said Gorgo.

"That's not going to fool anyone." Emily looked up. The dogg now had a terrible fake beard and mustache.

"What kind of Stonemaster are you?" said Gorgo.

"The kind of Stonemaster who isn't a Stonemaster!"

"Well, could you concentrate, please?"

Emily scrunched up her face. *How am I ever going to get rid of this dogg?*

Just as she was thinking that, another icon seemed to present itself to her, an image that looked like a winged leopard playing with a ball. The runes underneath resolved into words:

PetPortalPotty

Emily pressed on the icon and it expanded out like a hologram.

A cat with orange fur and three eyes addressed her while alien flute music played in the background. "Hi! Thanks for using the PetPortalPotty apth! Tired of cleaning up after your pet?"

The 3-D image changed to an enormous creature on a leash doing its equally enormous business on the sidewalk of a fantastical city, delicate spires rising in the background.

"Ew," said Emily.

"With one tap, you can send your pet for a walk in an entirely different universe. And with an infinite number to choose from, you'll never run out, and no one will ever catch on!"

"That hardly seems responsible," said Emily.

"Who asked you?" said the three-eyed cat creature.

"What? I thought this was recorded!" said Emily.

"Just tap the mystic rune again, and your portal will be open," said Three Eyes brightly, and Emily started thinking that maybe it *was* just a recording. "Just remember to keep the portal open until your little cutie is ready to come back in. PetPortalPotty: Why clean up a mess, when someone else can?"

"That's awful."

"Oh, shut up, you."

"Hey!"

But the face had vanished.

"Do it," said Gorgo. "You open the portal, and I'll dispose of our friend."

"Fine." Emily tapped on the rune. She heard a brief *twoodle* of the alien flute music, and then what was unmistakably a hinged doggy door shimmered into existence in front of them, floating a few inches from the ground.

"That," said Emily, "is *way* too small."

"Oh, look who's complaining. Next time get the paid version," said the cat voice.

"Are you a magical recording or not?"

"Thank you for using PetPortalPotty!"

"I'll make it work," said Gorgo. Seizing the dogg by the scruff of its neck, Gorgo tore it loose from his arm and held it up, its face a few inches from his own. The dogg snarled and snapped and squirmed.

"Ahh," sighed Gorgo. "So cute."

Then he proceeded to forcibly stuff the dogg head-first through the door, shoving it through bit by bit while the borders of the door bulged outward and the dogg growled and yelped and struggled.

"When I get the last of it through," said Gorgo, pushing mightily on the dogg's rear end, "you close that apth, or it's gonna try to come right back." Then Gorgo gave one final shove and the dogg disappeared from view. "Close it!" said Gorgo, holding the doggy door shut. From the other side came howls and scraping as the dogg fought to return. Emily tapped the icon. The door evaporated and the night was quiet again.

"Okay," said Gorgo, slapping his hands together like a workman finishing a job. "That's that."

"Where did the dogg go?"

"Who knows? You heard the apth. Some random dimension."

"Do you think it'll be okay?"

"You're concerned about it?"

"It just somehow felt a little cruel."

"Sure, cruel to whoever lives on the other side of that door. It's a dogg. It'll be fine. Unless it runs into a doggg," Gorgo added. "Then it'll be in trouble. Anyway. What's next?"

What was next? The wedding! Her family!

"I have to get back to the wedding!"

"A wedding? Ooh! I love weddings! Is there dancing?"

"You can't come!"

"Oh, thanks a lot," Gorgo said, then fumed to no one in particular, "You know, would it have been terrible to have a master who was fun?"

"Would it have been terrible not to have a super-natural servant who plans to eat me?" said Emily to the same no one. "Gorgo, I need to get back to the wedding reception, and to do that, I need to get up there." She pointed to the top of the cliff.

"Ooookay," said Gorgo.

"What are you doing? What are you dooooooiiiii—"

said Emily, because now she was sailing straight upward along the cliff face, Gorgo having grabbed her around the waist and launched her above his head.

"—iiiiiiing," continued Emily as the rock face raced by, and then *thup!* She landed gently on her feet on the edge of the cliff. Gorgo had thrown her with such accuracy that when she'd started coming down again, she had less than a foot to fall. A moment later he landed next to her with a barely discernible *thud*.

"You could have warned me," said Emily.

"Uh-huh. If I'd said, 'Hey, I'm going to throw you several hundred feet up to the top of this cliff,' what would you have said?"

"Um . . ."

"Right. You need to learn to trust me."

"Trust you? You keep promising to eat me."

"Trust me, I will. Now, you're sure I can't come to the wedding?"

"Absolutely not. You need to get right back in here," she said, holding up the Stone.

"Hold on. Before you force me back in there, can I make a suggestion?"

"Does it involve the spices and seasonings I should use to make myself tasty?"

"See, there you go! You're starting to enjoy the humor of the situation!"

"Believe me, I'm not. What's your suggestion?"

"My suggestion is this: Someone, or some*thing*, wants that Stone of yours. Someone powerful enough to send a shade through who knows how many dimensions to find it, and then a dogg to fetch it. You need to know who that someone is. Or *what*. Working an enchantment like that—sending a creature to a world it shouldn't be in—leaves tracks, sort of like magical footprints. But they're already starting to fade—I can feel it. So if you want to figure out who sent the dogg, you'd better do it now."

"Why should I care who did it?"

"Because I guarantee you, they'll try again, and next time will be worse."

"But I don't know how."

"But you're a Stonemaster."

"Stop saying that! I'm *not* a Stonemaster. I'm Emily Edelman, and I'm twelve years old, and I didn't ask for any of this, and I want it to go away!"

Gorgo was quiet for a moment. "Yeah . . . how's that working out for you?" he said.

Emily stared at him.

"All right, all right," she said testily, and held the Stone up again. Apths swam before her eyes, a galaxy of them, overwhelming her. How would she ever figure out who sent the dogg?

"You'd better hurry," said Gorgo. "The smell is fading."

"I'm *trying!*"

She did her best to focus her mind. *Who sent the dogg? Who worked that magic?*

"Hurry . . ."

"Gorgo."

An apth floated forward.

"Gorgo, have you ever heard of an apth called Snifftr? There's just an image of a big nose."

"Nothing else?"

"Wait, it says . . ."

Emily squinted at the runes, then rolled her eyes. "Pick me."

"So pick it!"

"Okay, okay," said Emily. She touched the image and the nose expanded into three dimensions, the way the cat had done. "I can't believe I'm doing this," Emily muttered, and inserted a finger into one of the nostrils. The instant she did the nose disappeared—and suddenly she heard loud snuffling and sniffing and had the impression that she was being gently attacked by two vacuum cleaners, one on each side of her face.

"Hey, what's—"

Then her vision was briefly blocked, and for an instant she thought she was looking up two enormous nostrils, one covering each of her eyes, and then she could see again and the snuffling noises were moving away from her.

"I must have screwed up again," she groaned.

"No—hee hee!" said Gorgo. "I think it's—hee hee! —the spell—hee hee hee! Stop it! Hee hee hee! That—hee hee—tickles—HEE HEE HEE!"

He was dancing in place, giggling, swatting ineffectually at something.

"They *are* nostrils!" said Emily.

And indeed they were: disembodied nostrils with no nose, busily sniffing up and down Gorgo's body, flitting back now to take more sniffs of Emily, each nostril about the size of a saucer. Emily could see now that they were visible only when they were positioned so that you were looking up them—but once they started sniffing the ground, which they were doing now, they couldn't be seen. Emily could still hear them, though, and detect the movement of the leaves and dirt with each in- and exhalation.

The nostrils were moving away from them now, and then they disappeared over the side of the cliff. "Is that it? Are they gone?" said Emily, but a moment later the snuffling noise returned, and she caught a glimpse of the nostrils as they crested the cliff. Then the sniffing got closer again and Emily got another unwanted view straight up the enormous nostrils. They appeared perfectly three-dimensional. They also appeared disgusting.

"This is so gross," said Emily.

"What's gross about it?" said Gorgo. The nostrils were sniffing him again. "You complain too much. I don't find it gross at all."

Then suddenly the nostrils sneezed: "AAAA-CHOOO!" Massively. Directly on Gorgo.

Gorgo looked down at his midsection. "Yyyyyyuck," he said. "It *is* gross."

The nostrils and sniffing had disappeared. But the evidence of the giant sneeze remained, in a gloppy, glistening blast pattern on Gorgo's chest.

"You're right," he said. "You must have screwed up. Blech." He reached to wipe off the mess.

"Wait!" said Emily.

"What? Why?!"

"I see something!"

She drew closer to him, brow furrowed, staring at the glow that was beginning on his chest. And then suddenly, there it was: a moving image.

"It's like looking at a screen," she said.

"Great. A screen made of magic snot," said Gorgo.

"Shh!"

The image wavered, blurred, then resolved. A torrential downpour. Nighttime. Emily could hear the rain. Lightning crackled, illuminating a structure, a terrifying building.

"Is there a thunderstorm happening on my chest?" said Gorgo.

"Quiet!"

Emily was inside the building now, peering into the darkest and gloomiest and least comfortable room she had ever seen. There was an overabundance of spiky objects and drippy candles and portraits of people with expressions on their faces that said, *I may be long dead and gone—but I'm still watching you and I don't like you!* A fire flickered in a freestanding fireplace made out of the massive blackened skull of some monstrous creature. The flames were greenish, a shade that reminded Emily of the dogg's eyes. All the furniture maintained the spiky and uncomfortable theme and was upholstered in what Emily *hoped* was animal hide and not something more sinister.

"What do you see?" said Gorgo. "In your mucus-vision."

"Some sort of scary room. Wait—I'm moving closer to what looks like a desk. There's something on it. It's . . ."

She paused, her expression confused.

"It's what? What is it?"

"It looks like . . . a *catalog*. Like a normal catalog you'd order stuff from. But . . . *weird* stuff. Wait—now I can see the mailing address: 'The Venomüch Family.' Uh-oh—someone is coming in!"

The image snapped back to a wide view of the room.

". . . the dogg should be back by now!" a man was saying.

"The Stonemaster must have defeated him," said the woman with him.

Emily watched the Venomüch family enter the room. She didn't need to be told that she should be afraid of these people.

"Now how will we find the Stone?" said the boy.

"It may be beyond our power," said the father. "Perhaps we—"

He stopped suddenly, as if he was listening. Emily caught her breath.

"Dad?" said the girl, but the father held up a hand for silence. Then his head turned until he was looking directly at Emily, and Emily felt a burst of terror.

"*I see you*," he said.

The wife was looking at her too. "Yes," said the woman. "Yes, I see you too . . . *Emily Edelman!*" Her voice rose to a shriek. "We'll get you, my prett—"

Emily shook her head and waved a hand as if she were brushing away a hornet, and the image vanished.

"You're shaking," said Gorgo. "You okay?"

"No," said Emily. "I don't think I am."

When Emily returned to the wedding reception, her mother saw her and nearly screamed. "Where have you been? What have you been doing?" she exclaimed. "Rolling in the dirt? Look at your clothes! They're ruined! Honestly, Emily, and you want us to treat you more like a grownup."

Emily didn't say a word the whole way home.

Emily lay in bed that night with the light on again, thinking. Then she got up, sat at her desk, and made a list, carefully considering each item as she wrote it down. When she was done, she summoned Gorgo. He unfolded, spotted the paper in her hand, and said, "Uh-oh."

"I have a list of rules," she said.

"Oh, boy."

"First off: I command you to always be honest with me."

"Okay. You're too old to have superhero bed sheets," he said. "What? You said I have to be honest."

"You know what I mean. And the sheets are *ironic*."

"Of course they are. But yes, fine, I'll be honest with you."

"Two: you have to protect me."

"I am. I'm trying to protect you against foolish bedding decisions. Okay, okay," he added when she glared at him again. "Didn't I protect you against the dogg?"

"You said you would have let me fall."

He thought about that.

"Okay, that's true. Yes, I pledge to protect you."

"Okay. Three: no hurting or eating anyone."

"Anyone? What if they're trying to hurt you?"

"Then you must endeavor to protect me without harming them."

Gorgo reached out and took the paper from her. "I thought so. You actually wrote that out: 'You must endeavor . . .'"

"Yes I did," Emily said, and snatched the paper back from him.

"And what else?" he said.

"That's it. For now."

Gorgo nodded, evidently reviewing the list in his mind. "That's pretty good," he said. "You went with general rules as opposed to specifics, which can be easier to twist. Well done, Stonemaster."

"I'm not a—"

He held up a hand. "I know, I know. But on that topic, I've been thinking. I have an idea of someone who might be able to help you."

"What? Who?"

"You're not going to believe me."

CHAPTER
EIGHT

Y ou were right, Gorgo. I don't believe you," said
Emily in a low voice as they walked through the school
halls. He was in the Stone, which was in her backpack, which was slung over one shoulder. It was Monday.
Classes had just ended, kids pulling belongings from their
lockers and getting ready to head home. The day had been
full of odd stares and fake burps and vicious smirking
from Kristy Meyer. At lunch Emily had sat alone at a table. She saw Angela Rodriguez, holding a tray, approach-
ing her uncertainly. *No way*, thought Emily. She got up and
left.

"Gorgo," said Emily now, "are you sure about this?"

"It's worth a try," Gorgo said.

"I guess. But I'm not exactly sure how I'm supposed to

start the conversation. 'Hi, I'm Emily, and I have this problem . . .'"

"Who are you talking to?"

Oh, no. Kristy's voice, coming from right behind her.

"I'm just talking to myself," said Emily.

"You're so weird," said Kristy, drawing even with her. She was alone this time. Emily wondered how long Kristy had been following behind her, listening. "Why are you so weird? Is it because you're such a loser? Or are you a loser because you're weird? Probably both, right?"

Smirk. Kristy turned to go, her mission accomplished.

"Well, at least I'm not an awful excuse for a human being who uses cruelty to cover up her own insecurities."

It was Gorgo, in a pretty fair approximation of Emily's voice.

Kristy spun back, her face reddening in fury. "What did you say?" she demanded.

"Nothing!" said Emily.

"Oh, you are so going to get it! If you think life is rough now, just you wait!" said Kristy, and stalked off.

"Gorgo!" said Emily in a strangled voice. "Why did you do that?"

"What? You said to protect you!"

Gorgo kept defending himself, Emily shushing him,

until they came to their destination. Emily paused outside the door. LIBRARY, said the sign.

"Are you *sure* about this?" said Emily again.

When Gorgo had told her he knew of someone who might be able to help her, she hadn't expected him to say, "You have to talk to the school Librarian."

"How is the librarian going to know?"

"Not the 'librarian.' The *Librarian*." Just like when he said "Stone," Gorgo said "Librarian" in a manner that made the capital letter unmistakable.

"Fine. How is the . . . *Librarian* going to know?"

What followed was a long explanation about how libraries—particularly *school* libraries—are magical nexus, neutral territories for all the different domains in the multiverse.

"And Librarians are the masters of these neutral territories," said Gorgo. "In fact, I've heard of one Librarian who's an orangutan, but who can—"

"A what?"

"Never mind. My point is, we should talk to the Librarian."

Now, standing outside the library door, Emily was feeling foolish. The library had been her favorite place in her old school. She loved to search the shelves for new books, then curl up in one of the chairs or just sit on the carpeted floor and read. So yes, a school library had always seemed like a magical place to her, but *that* kind of magical?

"You going in or what?" said Gorgo.

Emily went in.

The Clearview School library looked like most school libraries: walls lined with shelves; rows of standing shelves that were themselves like walls; an area with a motley collection of comfy kid-size chairs for reading; a few long desks surrounded by less comfortable chairs. The comfy and noncomfy chairs were about half-occupied by students with their noses in books or homework.

The librarian—or *Librarian*—sat at her desk, which itself sat toward the back of the room, giving her a commanding view of the long desks and reading area. She was younger than Emily had expected, and prettier, an African American woman with very dark skin and close-cropped hair who Emily guessed was in her early thirties. Despite her apparent youth, she had reading glasses perched on her nose, her head tilted back slightly so she could see through them as she perused a book.

Emily went and stood in front of the Librarian's desk. There was a nameplate on it that said MS. HALLGREN. Ms. Hallgren did not seem to notice her.

"Um . . . excuse me," said Emily shyly.

Ms. Hallgren, without glancing up from her book, said, "Yes?"

"May I speak with you?"

"Listening."

When Emily didn't say anything, Ms. Hallgren looked up.

"You don't seem to be talking."

"No, ma'am."

Ms. Hallgren examined Emily more closely, inclining her head so that she could see over her glasses.

"You're the new girl, aren't you?"

"Yes, ma'am," said Emily. Then she quickly added, "I didn't try to burn down the auditorium."

"Yes, I heard that was quite a magic trick."

Emily paused, wondering if she had detected a bit of emphasis on "magic" or had imagined it. She looked around at the kids sitting at the desks and in the chairs. Then she leaned in a bit closer and said in a low voice, "Ms. Hallgren, can I talk to you in private?"

"In private?"

"Yes."

"I can't just leave the library. Or kick everyone out."

At that moment, Gorgo's irritated voice came out of Emily's backpack, loud enough that Emily was afraid the other kids would hear it: "Hey, could we speed this up, already?"

Emily knew that Ms. Hallgren must have heard him. But Ms. Hallgren's expression didn't change. She just stared at Emily, not moving. Emily gazed back, holding her breath.

A long moment passed.

Then Ms. Hallgren abruptly stood up and clapped her hands.

"Okay, kids," she announced. "Library's closed! Everyone out! Out, out, out!"

She marched up and down the line of shelves, shooing kids toward the exit as she went. When the last of the kids had filed out, grumbling— "Why does *she* get to stay?" "That's not your concern!"—Ms. Hallgren locked the door, then sat down behind her desk once again and regarded Emily for another long moment.

"What's your name?" she said.

"Emily Edelman, ma'am."

"Well, Emily Edelman, why do you have what sounds to me very much like an evil creature from the lowest depths in your backpack?"

"The 'lowest depths'?" came Gorgo's indignant voice. "Do you know how much the real estate costs there?"

"I'm not talking to you!" said Ms. Hallgren.

"I mean, we have a very nice *view* of the lowest depths, but—"

"Hush!"

"Sorry."

"Emily?" said Ms. Hallgren.

"I don't know! That's why I'm here!" said Emily, and then everything came out in a rush: "I was on the beach and I found this thing and then there was the magic show and then there was this daw-guh-guh—"

"All right, all right," said Ms. Hallgren, holding up her hands. "What 'thing'?"

Emily unzipped her backpack, pulled out the Stone, and placed it on Ms. Hallgren's desk.

"Aha," said Ms. Hallgren quietly, drawing back a bit. She didn't touch the Stone or move much, other than to carefully adjust her reading glasses so she could better peer at it. She seemed, to Emily, like someone in the presence of something that might explode.

Still without touching the Stone, Ms. Hallgren leaned back a bit more so she could open the wide, flat drawer in front of her, from which she produced what looked like a common, everyday ID card. Then, with a certain amount of ceremony, she held the card up and announced, as if addressing a panel of judges, "I hereby present my Library card and state that I am a duly authorized Librarian." Emily could once again hear the capital *L*. "As such, I exercise my right in this neutral zone to examine this magical artifact with no interference from outside powers, good or evil."

"So it's true," whispered Emily. "It's true about libra—Librarians."

"Of course it's true," said Ms. Hallgren crisply, returning the card to the drawer and shutting it. "But that will remain our secret. Can you imagine the chaos that would result if students knew that libraries were magical places and if they understood the true role of Librarians? But enough of that. Let's take a look."

Gently lifting the Stone from the desk, Ms. Hallgren turned it in her hands to examine it from all angles, mm-hmm-ing and aha-ing to herself. After about a minute, she gently placed the Stone back onto her desk.

"This, Emily, is a very rare and *very* powerful—and I might add, very *dangerous*—item. This is a Mobile Spellstone."

"I told her that," said Gorgo.

"Ah, yes," said Ms. Hallgren. "And then there's our friend."

"Hi," said Gorgo. "Can I come out now?"

Ms. Hallgren looked at Emily. "You've summoned this creature?"

"Yes."

"All right, let's see it," she said.

"Abrakadonkulous," said Emily.

"Aaaahhhh," said Gorgo after he did his unfolding thing, stretching his limbs. "Much better."

"State your name," said Ms. Hallgren.

"Baelmadeus Gorgostopheles Lacrimagnimum Turpisatos Metuotimo Dolorosum Tenebris Morsitarus, ma'am," he said.

"You were imprisoned in this Stone?"

"Yes, ma'am."

"And I assume you are bound to serve its owner?"

"Yes'm."

"And I further assume that your servitude will continue until you are somehow freed, at which point I also assume you intend to devour your master—in this case, Emily?"

"Uh . . . yes. Yes, ma'am. That is, in fact, uh, the plan."

"Mm-hmm," said Ms. Hallgren, gazing at him disapprovingly.

"What?" said Gorgo. "What do you expect? I mean, look at me."

"I'd prefer not to. Emily, do you know why you came into possession of this Stone?"

"No."

"Are you perhaps the seventh daughter of—"

"I'm not the seventh anything of anything," said Emily.

"We've already been through this," put in Gorgo.

"Well, no matter. What matters is this: You, Emily Edelman, are now the proud owner of this incredibly powerful and dangerous item. It is bound to you, and you to it. Not to mention that you are now coincidentally the unwilling master of an evil creature from the lowest—"

"Mid," inserted Gorgo.

"*Mid*depths, who must obey your commands for now but will make a minor snack of you at its earliest possible convenience."

"Oh, great, make me feel *bad* about it," said Gorgo.

"I will speak with you in a moment," said Ms. Hallgren. "And put down that book—it's smoldering."

Gorgo hastily put down a picture book that was indeed starting to smoke.

"Sorry," he said. "I get a little nervous around Librarians."

"Ms. Hallgren," said Emily, "someone tried to take

the Stone." Then she quickly told her about the dogg and the Venomüch family.

"I see," Ms. Hallgren said. She carefully handed the Stone back to Emily, then stood up. "Come with me."

Emily followed her, Gorgo trailing behind, to a small, ornate bookshelf made of dark wood.

"What's this?" said Emily.

"It's where we keep the magical volumes," said Ms. Hallgren. "Every school library has one—most students just never notice it. The more books you read, the more chances there are that you'll see it."

"Nice one," said Gorgo. "Clever bit of moral instruction there."

"Shush."

"Why don't you tell her how broccoli is a magic vegetable."

"Broccoli *is* a magic vegetable. Everyone knows that."

Ms. Hallgren crouched in front of the bookcase, running her finger along the spines of books as she searched for one particular title.

"Let's see . . . *Spell Hacks Everyone Should Know*, no . . . *Curses Cured: Core Curriculum*, nope . . . *Enchantments with Broccoli*, no . . . Aha. Here we go."

With some effort Ms. Hallgren pulled a very thick

leather-bound book off the shelf and set it down with a thump on top of the bookcase. On the cover in embossed gold writing was the title: *A Veritable Who's Who of Prominent Magical Families.*

"What's that?" said Gorgo.

"It's a veritable who's who of . . ." began Ms. Hallgren. "You get the idea."

She opened it and began flipping through it. Emily caught glimpses of coats of arms and family crests and text handwritten with a quill and ink. "Vaaaaaaan, Vantl, Veber . . . aha. Venomüch."

There was a descriptive paragraph written in old-fashioned writing underneath a coat of arms overflowing with hydras and other vicious-looking creatures. When Emily leaned forward for a closer look, they started snapping and striking at her.

"Whoa!"

"All right then!" said Ms. Hallgren, slamming the book shut. She turned to Emily, her expression grave. "Emily, I don't need to tell you what would happen if creatures like the Venomüches came into possession of a Stone like yours. It would be a disaster. And whether you want the responsibility or not, it's your duty as a Stonemaster to prevent that from happening."

"But that's just it: I'm *not* a Stonemaster! I don't even really know how to use this thing!"

"Have you read the user's manual?"

"I didn't even know there *was* one!"

"Hold on a moment."

Grimacing with effort, Ms. Hallgren lifted the *Who's Who* and placed it back onto the shelf. Then she ran her finger along more spines until she located a very thin volume and pulled it out. It was barely thicker than a comic book.

"User's manual. Come with me," she said, and Emily and Gorgo once again filed after her until they reached one of the shared tables.

"Hopefully this will be sturdy enough," said Ms. Hallgren, eyeing the long desk.

"Sturdy enough?" said Emily. "For that?"

"Yes," said Ms. Hallgren, and placed the booklet onto the table.

Emily blinked.

"You've got to be kidding me," she said.

A moment ago the thin booklet had been, well, a thin booklet. Now, however, Emily was looking at the most absurdly thick book she had ever seen. It was like the pages of a dozen of the thickest dictionaries stacked atop one another, mocking the cover that tried to contain them. It was less a book than a rectangular pillar, the top cover so high it was even with Emily's nose.

The table, which was bowing slightly in the middle, creaked ominously.

"*That's* the user's manual?" said Emily.

"I'm afraid so," said Ms. Hallgren. "Here—I'm usually telling students *not* to do this, but why don't you stand on this chair."

Emily did, bringing her to a height that allowed her to open the cover. Which led to another, equally unpleasant discovery.

At first glance she thought that the page was simply covered with gray-black blocks. But looking closer she realized that those blocks were indeed made up of letters, letters in type so small and dense it merely appeared to be a uniform mass.

"Oh, dear," Emily said.

"Take these," said Ms. Hallgren, offering Emily her reading glasses.

"Um . . . will these work for me?" said Emily. "We probably don't have the same prescription."

"They're Librarian reading glasses, Emily. They'll let you read anything."

Emily took them, gingerly put them on, then looked down at the book. It said:

> Congratulations on your acquisition of a Mobile Spellstone, if you haven't already been skewered, dissolved, cubed, puréed, turned to stone, turned to sand, turned into a sandwich, turned into a turnip, and/or eaten! Please be sure to read all of these instructions, as improper (and even proper) use of the Mobile Spellstone can be exceedingly perilous and cause many serious consequences (please see appendices 1479–2562, "Lists of Very Serious Consequences," and the appendices to the appendices, "Lists of Even Worse Consequences," as well as the supplemental insert, *"Nooooooo!"*).

"How am I ever going to read all of this?" said Emily.

"It does seem rather daunting," admitted Ms. Hallgren.

"Really? It doesn't seem that bad to me," said Gorgo, reaching out a claw.

"No, don't—" began Ms. Hallgren.

There was a very bright flash and a sound like *FWOOOF*.

"—touch that," finished Ms. Hallgren.

When the colored blobs stopped dancing in front of her eyes, Emily realized that there was now a pile of ashes on the table.

"Oops?" said Gorgo.

"Now what am I going to do?" wailed Emily.

"Well, at least you don't have to read it," submitted Gorgo hopefully.

"There is a dustpan and a broom over there in the corner," said Ms. Hallgren to him.

"Yes, ma'am," he said politely, and went to fetch them.

"Ms. Hallgren, what am I supposed to do? You have to help me!"

"I'm afraid I can't, Emily. The rules are very strict. Helping you any further would be a violation."

"Can I just hide in here forever? Isn't this, like, a safe zone?"

"I wish you could, Emily. But that, too, would be a violation."

"So what do I do? I feel completely alone!"

"You have to learn how to use the Stone properly. You have to become a true Stonemaster. And unfortunately, I don't think you have much time to do it. But you *have to learn*, do you understand me?"

"Yes, ma'am. But how?"

"You'll just have to do it by what we call trial and terror."

"You mean 'trial and *error*,' right?" said Emily.

"Umm, sure. That, too," said Ms. Hallgren.

Ms. Hallgren gazed after Emily as the girl left the library, the door closing behind her.

"Poor kid," said Ms. Hallgren aloud to the empty room. "I wish I could help her. I hope *someone* does, because she's going to need all the help she can get if she is to succeed. And she'd better succeed, for her sake." She paused, then added, "For all our sakes."

Then she gathered her belongings, shut off the lights in the library, and locked the door behind her as she left. She had little doubt that the occupant remaining in the library would quickly figure out that the door could be opened from the inside. Still, when Ms. Hallgren had rounded the corner down the hall, she waited a bit until she heard it: the sound of the library door being gently opened again and then eased shut, followed by footsteps receding down the hallway.

Ms. Hallgren smiled and went on her way.

CHAPTER
NINE

When Emily got home, Hilary was parked barefoot in one of the armchairs in the living room. Their mother had started her new job, so Hilary had to babysit each afternoon until one of the parents came home. Which suited Hilary just fine, because that meant she could text to her heart's content. She was doing that now, using her pinkies because she had essentially burned out every other finger.

"I'm home," said Emily.

Hilary briefly unstuck her eyes from the screen.

"What's wrong with you? You look awful," she said.

"Nothing. I'm just worried about a few things," said Emily.

"What do *you* have to worry about? You have *no idea*

what it's like to worry. Jennifer is back with Alex, and Alex's brother Eric is now, like, totally blowing up my phone, and then there's this cute guy who . . ."

Emily sighed while complicated details of interpersonal relationships streamed past her. Every so often Hilary's phone would ping and she'd quickly read something and text back, her monologue hardly slowing.

"That sounds terrible," Emily said, when Hilary had come to what seemed like a potential stopping point. "Where's Dougie?"

"Dunno. I think he's downstairs or something."

On cue, Emily heard a smashing sound, followed by giggles. "Oops!" said Dougie from the basement.

"Maybe you should check on him?" suggested Emily.

"I'm sure he's fine," said Hilary. There was another crash. "Oops!" said Dougie again. Emily wasn't sure what was getting broken downstairs, but she knew she'd somehow be blamed for it.

"Sounds like you have it all under control," she said to Hilary. "I'm going to go up to my room and do my homework."

Hilary didn't answer, her attention once again on her phone.

When Emily got to her room, she closed the door,

sat on the bed, and took out the Stone. *You have to learn,* Ms. Hallgren had said. Fine. She would learn. She'd practice, and she'd learn.

"Awaken," she said.

"What are you doing out there?" came Gorgo's voice.

"Practicing."

"Good idea," he said. "But be careful. Remember, 'Pride goeth before—'"

"'A fall,'" Emily concluded.

"Is that the saying in your world?" said Gorgo. "Where I'm from, it's 'Pride goeth before a series of huge unintended explosions and lightning bolts and the accidental transformation of yourself into a filbert.'"

"Either way, it doesn't matter," said Emily. "I don't have any pride."

She focused on the Stone's screen and swiped her way past endless apths. What should she try? What would be something relatively harmless to experiment with? She did more swiping. Her concentration kept being broken by the annoying whine of the hedge trimmer that Mr. Petersen was using in his backyard. She did her best to ignore it, but the sound was pitched just right to penetrate the walls of both the house and her skull. *I wish he'd stop,* she thought.

Then: aha—what's this? A tiny owl was owl-scowling at Emily from the screen. She focused on the runes under the apth, which transformed themselves into FURIOUS AVIANS. The apth seemed like a game. A game! That would be harmless. *Let's try it,* Emily thought. Outside, the hedge trimming continued. How annoying.

Still irritated by the noise from next door, she touched the icon and felt the tiny thrill of a spell taking effect. But then nothing happened.

"Huh," she said.

"You try something?" said Gorgo.

"I don't think it worked."

Except it had.

Outside in his backyard, Mr. Petersen had a moment to register that it had suddenly gotten much darker, and then another brief moment to wonder if a cloud had passed in front of the sun and if it was going to rain. And then he was surrounded by a squawking, flapping, pecking nightmare, as ten thousand very upset sparrows—furious avians, you might say—swarmed about him as if he were a predator trying to rob their nests.

In her room, Emily furrowed her brow and examined the Stone. She was aware at some level that the hedge trimmer had stopped, for which she was thankful. She wished all those birds would stop their excited chirping, though.

Mr. Petersen was flying. Or, more accurately, was being flown, lifted into the air by the swarm of determined birds.

"AAAAHH!!!" he shouted, but as he was surrounded by several layers of birds, it came out as "AAAAHH!"

Emily, her back to her window, heard an odd rustling noise pass rapidly behind her. She turned, but there was nothing. She shrugged.

"Did you hear someone screaming?" said Gorgo.

"I don't think so," she said.

"Maybe you should stop whatever it is you're doing?"

Emily shrugged again. Whatever the apth did, it didn't seem to do it very well. She touched the icon and willed the program to shut down.

Abruptly released by his avian escort, Mr. Petersen plummeted to the ground and landed roughly on top of his compost pile.

"Okay," said Emily, doing some more swiping. "What's next? Hey, look at this!" she said, delighted to have found something she recognized.

"What is it?" asked Gorgo.

"I think it's a book. A really famous one."

She tapped on the apth. Part of her mind was still on Mr. Petersen—he sure gave her suspicious looks whenever she walked past.

At that moment Mr. Petersen was staggering into his house. He wasn't quite sure what had happened, but it seemed to have involved a lot of birds. *Maybe,* he thought, *maybe I just fell and bumped my head.* Because it didn't seem likely that he had actually been picked up and flown in several circuits around his house. *I must have bumped my head,* he thought. *Especially because I'm now hallucinating that there's a very furry werewolf sitting at a potter's wheel in my living room, crafting a mug.*

Back in her bedroom, Emily couldn't figure out what had happened after she'd touched the second apth. As far as she could tell, nothing. "Well, that didn't seem to work either," she said. Anyway, she now realized that her previous excitement had been misplaced—she had misread the name of the second apth. The runes had spelled HAIRY POTTER, not what she had initially thought. She shut that apth down too.

In Mr. Petersen's living room, the hairy pottery-making werewolf suddenly disappeared in a puff of blue smoke.

Emily looked for something else. *Ah, here's one,* she thought. *Another game.*

"'Crushed by Candy,'" she read out loud.

"I wouldn't," said Gorgo.

"Shh."

Mr. Petersen, in his dazed state, decided that perhaps he should go out for a walk around the block. That would do it. For some reason, though, he first picked up the mug that was lying on the carpet and examined it. The ceramic piece had remained behind when the werewolf and potter's wheel had suddenly vanished. Mr. Petersen carefully placed the mug on the fireplace mantel. It was a nice mug.

I'm sure there's a rational explanation for all of this, he thought. Then he stepped out his front door, just in time to see his car get buried under several tons of brightly colored candy.

Emily heard the crash and went to her window. She could see Mr. Petersen standing in his driveway. She could also see what he was gaping at.

"Uh-oh," she said.

Angela Rodriguez, standing a few doors down from Mr. Petersen's house, took out her notebook and added some notes to what she had labeled "The Emily Edelman File."

— Mr. Petersen surrounded by dense cloud of birds, lifted into air, flown around house. Birds then leave, she wrote.

— Approximately five minutes later, Mr. Petersen comes out front door. Just then giant pile of candy appears from nowhere and covers his car.

— Swarm of birds returns. Each bird takes piece of candy and flies away until there is no more candy. Mr. Petersen now holding head and looking at car, which has been crushed nearly flat by the candy.

Angela then watched the three Edelman children emerge from their house to observe Mr. Petersen. She wrote down in her notebook that Emily appeared particularly agitated.

You might think that Angela herself might be disturbed or frightened by the scene. Then again, she'd already overheard and witnessed some pretty unusual things earlier in the day, when she'd been hiding in the library during Emily's discussion with Ms. Hallgren. There was a nook at the back of the library where it was easy to conceal yourself, which she had done when Ms. Hallgren was shooing everyone out. Then Angela had silently crept out and found a spot behind one of the shelves where she could peer wide-eyed through a gap in the books at the unfolding scene and excitedly scribble down her impressions.

When Gorgo made his appearance, she'd had to clap a hand over her mouth to muffle a whimper of fear and surprise. But her reaction was very different when Ms. Hallgren led Emily over to the bookcase of magical tomes. In fact, what Angela wrote in her notebook at that point was

I KNEW IT.

Then she wrote

RESOLVED: MUST SPEAK WITH EMILY.

Quite a crowd was gathered to watch the tow truck hoist Mr. Petersen's car up onto the flatbed in preparation for transporting the ruined vehicle away. Even Hilary came outside, if only to take pictures and post them online.

Emily didn't watch. She went back inside, up the stairs, into her room, and into her closet. Then she closed the door and sat on the floor and hugged her knees to her chest.

"How's the practice session going?" asked Gorgo from inside the Stone.

"Not so good," said Emily.

She wasn't sure how long she would have stayed in there if the doorbell hadn't rung. She ignored the first ring, and the second. And the third and fourth. When it became an insistent chiming, she finally went downstairs. Hilary was out back, texting. Dougie was in the basement, probably breaking things. The doorbell rang again. Emily jerked open the front door.

"We need to talk," said Angela Rodriguez.

Emily shut the door in her face.

The doorbell rang again, then rang several times more.

Emily opened the door a crack.

"What do you want?" she said.

"I was in the library," said Angela. "I heard everything."

Emily slammed the door again and leaned against it, panting.

The doorbell rang again, then again.

"Emily," said Angela, crouching down to speak through the mail slot, "I think I can help you."

There was a pause. Then the door opened again, ever so slightly. Emily peeked through the one-inch aperture.

"Help me how?"

"I've read the user's manual."

CHAPTER
TEN

I don't think I have any special powers or anything like that," said Angela. "I just like to read."

She and Emily and Gorgo were seated on the floor in Emily's room, eating from a bowl of tortilla chips and sipping on juice boxes (Hilary, watching Emily go upstairs with Angela, had said, "Why do you need *three* juice boxes?" "Just because," said Emily). After a single whispered "wow" and a headshake after Gorgo had emerged in the bedroom, Angela seemed to have adjusted to his threatening appearance. Something about Angela, thought Emily, made her think of the term *unflappable*.

Angela took a sip of her juice now and said, "I spend a lot of time in the library. After a while I started noticing this dark wooden shelf that I'd never seen before. So I started reading those books too, all these weird books about magic and enchantments. I thought it was some sort of joke, until today."

"And you read that whole gigantic user's manual?" asked Emily.

"No, it didn't transform like that for me. It stayed small, just a few pages long. Like one of those quick guides that tell you about the important parts. I read that."

"So you know what all these things are?" said Emily, holding up the Stone to show Angela the apths.

"Wait—to me it just looks like a stone," said Angela. "I can't see what you see. But is there a moon in the upper right-hand corner?"

"Yes. But it's just a sliver now. And everything seems dimmer or something."

"Well, have you been charging the Stone?"

"Charging it? How do I do that?"

"You have to leave it in the moonlight. And that little moon is like the battery indicator. From what I read, the Stone is like a phone—the more apths you use, the more power they take, and some take more power than others."

"What else?"

"Hold on."

Angela pulled out her memo pad and examined her notes.

"You know about m-post?"

"M-post?"

"Magic post. You know, electronic mail is e-mail, magic post is—"

"Got it."

"Lemme see. There's a mapping function that tells you how to travel to different spots in the multiverse, and something about a type of money that lets you pay for new apths, or upgrades, or whatever," said Angela. "It's called . . ." She referenced her notes. "TwitCoin. Have you heard of that?" she said to Gorgo.

"TwitCoin?" said Gorgo. "It's Twexellian Interrealm Tender. It's the most widely accepted currency across the multiverse."

Emily was frowning.

"What?" said Angela.

"This all helps, but I still don't know how to really use the Stone and all the apths."

"Here's the thing," said Angela, indicating her notes again. "From what I read, it's all about *intention*. The guide kept talking about that, how the Stone has what it called 'inner voice recognition.' It knows what you want. If you concentrate, it will show you the apth you need. But the apth is just part of a spell—you have to focus your intention to direct the apth to work the way you want it to. I think the intention thing is pretty important. It kept saying how the Stonemaster has to stay focused on the goal."

"That's what happened to poor Mr. Petersen!" said Emily. "I was thinking of him when I was playing with those apths, and all that stuff happened! That was all my fault! You see? I'm *not* a Stonemaster."

"You've got to stop saying that," said Gorgo. "A little more practice and you're going to be a stone Stonemaster of that Stone, Master." He finished his juice with a gurgly slurp and then popped the whole box into his mouth.

There was a sudden pounding on the door, followed by laughter and running footsteps. Emily didn't bother to get up. It was the fourth time it had happened. She was used to this game.

"Ugh. I can't stand my little brother. Or my older sister."

"Really? I think you're lucky," said Angela. "At least it's not just you."

Emily realized that she didn't know anything about Angela—all this time, they had been talking about the Stone and nothing else.

"You don't have any brothers or sisters?"

"Nope. It's just me and my parents."

So they sat for another hour, talking about regular things: school, their families, other kids, what books and songs and activities they liked. Gorgo mostly stayed silent, content to eat the rest of the chips, the bag, and finally the bowl.

Chatting as if everything were normal, Emily felt for the first time as though she could breathe a little easier. As if she wasn't so alone.

"I guess I should get going," said Angela finally, standing up. Emily joined her.

"You should get going too," said Emily to Gorgo, pointing to the Stone.

"What? Can't I just go out for a walk sometime, do a little evil?"

"No. Get back in there."

"Fine, fine." He stood, towering over both of them, then reached out a hand to Angela. "Nice to meet you. I hope we can still be friends after I eat this one," he said, jerking a thumb at Emily.

"Uh . . ." said Angela.

"I'm kidding. I'll probably eat you, too."

Then he folded himself up and into the Stone.

Emily and Angela stood there awkwardly for a moment.

"Well, thanks for coming over," said Emily. "And for all the information."

"Sure."

They walked together downstairs and to the front door.

"Well," said Emily.

"Yeah. See you tomorrow, I guess."

"Yeah."

Angela walked down the front steps and started to cross the lawn.

"Hey," said Emily. Angela stopped and turned. "Thanks."

Angela smiled. "You're welcome," she said, then waved and turned again. Then stopped once more and turned back. "Emily?"

"Yes?"

"Be careful."

That night Emily carefully placed the Stone onto her windowsill and got into bed.

She couldn't sleep. How, she wondered, had she ever worried about anything before she found the Stone?

"Abrakadonkulous," she whispered quietly.

"Hey, kid," Gorgo said when he had unfolded.

"I can't sleep," said Emily.

"What's up?"

"Do you think those people, those Venomuck people or whatever, do you think they'll try something else?"

"Yep. No doubt."

Emily was quiet a moment.

"Gorgo," she said, "I'm scared."

"Yeah, I don't blame you," said Gorgo. He saw her expression. "Sorry. Look, go to sleep. I'll keep watch."

He sat down cross-legged, back against the wall.

"Really?" she said.

"Yup. I mean, I *am* your servant." He reached out to her bookshelf and pulled off a book. "Ooh, I love this series."

"You're not going to set it on fire, are you?"

"No — I'll be very careful."

Emily didn't know how he could read in the dark, but he seemed to be able to. She listened to him turning the pages, occasionally chuckling to himself, and she fell asleep.

When she woke up in the morning, he was still sitting against the wall.

"Morning," he said.

"Morning," she said.

There was a small pile of books around him. There was also a pile of something else.

"Gorgo?" said Emily. "What are those . . . *things?*"

They looked like massive spider legs, each three feet long, each ending in vicious pincers. They looked like they were made of metal.

"Oh, these?" said Gorgo. "Your friends sent another nasty visitor last night."

"What! What was it?"

Gorgo shook his head. "You don't want to know," he said. "It was, however, *delicious.*" He gestured to the remaining legs. "I'll have the rest for breakfast."

"Gorgo?"

"Yeah?"

"Thanks."

"Just doing as ordered, miss."

"The razor spider failed," said Maligno Sr.

"What?" said Acrimina.

"It failed. I told you it would," said Maligno.

BRRRRRRZZZZZZ! There was a loud and unpleasant grinding noise.

"Where is it now?" said Acrimina.

"Where? Somewhere in the digestive system of that demonic creature, I imagine."

BRRRRRRRRZZZZ!

They were on the back patio, sitting on recently ordered lawn furniture fashioned from spines and rib cages. The sun was barely visible through the sulfurous yellow dinge of the clouds overhead. The children were playing in the backyard, which featured a skull-shaped decorative pond and terrifying lawn ornaments and was contained by thick stone walls at least twenty feet high.

"We must bring the girl here, Maligno," said Acrimina.

"Yes, but how?"

"I have a—"

BRRRZZZZZZ!

"Children, please!" said Acrimina. "Turn off that toy! You can play with it later."

"Awww!" they said. Maligno Jr. switched off the My Li'l Woodchipper, into which he and Maligna had been gleefully feeding a series of fluffy stuffed animals.

"And even if we bring her here, how will we defeat her and get the Stone? The creature will protect her," said Maligno Sr.

"He will until he won't," said Acrimina.

"Ah," said Maligno.

"Exactly," said Acrimina. "We don't need to defeat *her*. All we need to do is free *him*. Razor spiders aren't the only things he'll eat."

They smiled at each other.

"So how do we get her here?" Maligno asked.

"I have a plan."

"I knew you would, my love."

CHAPTER
ELEVEN

When Emily got to school the next day, her locker had several stickers on it, the kind you put on your chest that say HELLO, MY NAME IS _____.
Instead of a name were words like LOSER and WEIRDO and FREAK, all in different styles of handwriting. Emily scratched at the stickers with her nails, but they were stuck tenaciously to the smooth metal of the locker, and she could get off only one thin strip at a time, leaving behind a rough layer of paper and adhesive. As the day went on, she realized that she shouldn't even bother, because every hour there were more and more nasty stickers slapped on by anonymous hands.

At lunch Angela came over with her tray and sat down and Emily nearly hugged her.

"Just ignore them," said Angela.

"That's what parents always say," said Emily.

"Yeah."

"You think it works?"

"Not really, no."

By the end of the day the surface of the locker door was nearly invisible: WEIRDO FREAK LOSER IDIOT UGGO LOSER LOSER LOSER, the insults literally piled one atop the other.

Angela helped her peel off a few of the more obscene ones. "Just let the janitor deal with the rest," she said.

"Do you want to come over today?" said Emily.

"Sure, yeah. I have chess club for an hour, but I can walk over after that."

"Great."

"Ma, I think I got one," said Maligno Jr., coming in the back door. He was holding a mushroom in his hand, a mushroom so toxic that if *you* were to pick it up in *your* hand, you'd be dead right . . . about . . . *now*.

Acrimina took the mushroom from her son and examined it closely, sniffing it. "It's certainly the right shape," she said, and held it up next to his ear while he giggled, because the mushroom did indeed resemble a disembodied (or dis-em-headed) ear. Then she brought it to her mouth and nibbled it experimentally. "Yes, this will do. Well done. Go be mean to your sister now."

"Yes, Ma!" He ran off. As Acrimina climbed the winding, crumbling stairway up to the high tower, she could hear the sounds of her children fighting each other with spiked clubs, and she smiled with warm pride.

She seated herself at the scarred wooden table in the center of the tower room, surrounded by skeletons and glass tubes and jars containing shocking things. Gently cradling the earlike mushroom in her hands and focusing her mind, Acrimina leaned forward and began to whisper cajoling words into it.

There are some very rare people who will never do a bad thing, no matter what the cost is to themselves, and will try to stop others from doing bad things.

Other people—most of us, really—won't *usually* do a bad thing, but might not always step up and put a stop to a bad thing when they see one happening.

Then, further down the scale, are those people—and there are too many of them—who will see a bad thing happening and say, *Well, everyone else is doing it, why not just join in?*

And then there are the people who will do a bad thing with barely any nudging at all.

People such as, say, Kristy Meyer.

She was not thinking in such philosophical terms as she walked away from school on that Tuesday with her posse of friends. She wasn't exactly sure what she was doing, or why, but when she came out of cheerleading practice and saw Angela Rodriguez leaving the school, she'd simply said, "Let's follow her."

Almost as though someone had whispered into her ear and told her to do it.

Her friends, sensing mischief in the air the way sharks sense blood in the water, fell in line. They were joined by some boys who were also drawn by the promise of trouble, the group losing in collective judgment as it gained in numbers.

Angela, walking alone on her way to Emily's house, was listening to music on her headphones. She wasn't aware of the pack stalking her.

There was a sour merriment in the group as the kids drew closer to her, anticipation growing. If you'd stopped and asked any single one of them, "What are you doing? What are you *planning* on doing?" not one of them would have been able to answer.

Far away in the high tower, Acrimina whispered and cajoled and instructed.

Angela was almost in Emily's front yard when the group attacked, hands punching and scratching at her and pushing her to the ground.

Emily was in her room when she heard the commotion: shouts, mean laughter, an indignant voice. Angela's voice.

She took the stairs two at a time. Hilary was slumped in her favorite chair. Her pinkies had started to hurt, so she was now texting using a pencil clasped between her teeth.

"What's going on out there?" said Emily.

Hilary glanced at her. "'Ow 'ould I 'ow?" she gritted out, and went back to texting.

Emily opened the front door. Out in the street Angela was surrounded by a wolf pack of kids. They were playing keep-away with her backpack, tossing it from one to another as Angela chased after it, pushing her when she got too close.

"Hey!" shouted Emily, and ran out to help.

The Stone was still upstairs on the windowsill.

In the high tower, Acrimina kept up her efforts but shifted her focus to another target.

．　．　．　．

Dougie was playing out back in the Edelmans' yard. He was positioning his cars and trucks on the patio for what would be a massive multivehicle pileup. Which was usually one of his favorite activities. Then, all of a sudden, it was *totally boring*. What would be interesting? Maybe Emily had something in her room . . . ?

For some reason Dougie went right to the strange stone sitting on Emily's windowsill. Almost as if someone was directing him to it. When he picked up the object, his eyes widened in surprise and delight at the glowing screen. What was this—Emily had a mobile phone?! How come he'd never seen it? And why did it look like a rock?

Who cared. It was cool.

A particular icon seemed to be trying to get his attention. CASTLE DEFENDER! it said in flashing letters. He tapped on the image.

"Cooooool."

He knew this kind of game: little figures storming across a field toward a castle, while the player tried to defend the structure—tapping on the screen to add fighters here, siege engines there, build up the bulwarks on this side . . . Sighing happily, Dougie settled in to play.

. . . .

A long way away, Acrimina Venomüch descended the stairs from the tower. She was tired but satisfied. The plan she had set in motion was working perfectly.

She joined her husband and children in what they called the dying room. They were gathered around a large bowl filled with something that looked like oil but was even darker. In it they could see Dougie playing with the Stone.

"He may not be her," said Acrimina to her husband, "but he is closely related enough that he can use the Stone. At least enough for our purposes."

"So he'll come here, Ma?" asked Maligna.

"Not at first," said Acrimina. "Too difficult. Too distant. But he'll go to a place from which we can fetch him. And that will be your task, my darlings." Her children giggled their hideous giggle.

"And once we have him . . ." said Maligno Sr.

"Yes," said Acrimina. "She and her creature will follow."

Emily had seen a nature special on TV where adolescent baboons fought one another viciously, and that's what Kristy and her friends seemed like now: wild-eyed and feral and mindless, their humanity gone. They laughed raucously as they pummeled and clawed and kicked at her and Angela as the two tried to get Angela's bag back.

"Stop it!" yelled Emily. "Give it back!"

"Give it back! Give it back!" they mocked.

"Don't give it to her!" said Kristy. Her eyes were gleaming slits. They scared Emily, those eyes.

This was all happening more or less in front of Mr. Petersen's house. He had stayed home from school that day, because he still felt somewhat unsteady as he tried to sort out what, exactly, had happened the day before. He'd spent a lot of time sitting in a chair, holding the werewolf-made mug in his hands and staring dumbly at it.

That's what he was doing now, but his thoughts kept being interrupted by some sort of ruckus happening outside. He decided to go take a look.

Oh, no, he thought when he opened his front door. *It's that dreadful Emily Edelman girl. What kind of trouble is she making now?*

When Emily saw Mr. Petersen, she shouted to him: "Mr. Petersen!"

All of the kids froze, a boy named Drew holding Angela's backpack.

"Hello, Emily," Mr. Petersen said politely. "What's going on out here?"

"Hi, Mr. Petersen!" said Kristy sweetly.

"Oh, hello, Kristy!" said Mr. Petersen, visibly brightening. "Are you all having fun?"

"Yes, we're just playing!" said Kristy.

"Wonderful! Well, carry on!" he said, and closed the door.

"Wait!" shouted Emily, but he was gone.

Kristy smiled viciously at her, and Emily took an involuntary step backwards, triumphant hatred radiating from Kristy almost like a physical wave.

"No one's going to help you," said Kristy quietly. "No one will ever be your friend. I control the school." She directed her gaze at Drew. "You!" she said, pointing at him. "Throw the bag in that tree!"

Without a moment's hesitation, Drew spun himself in a quick circle to gain momentum and hurled the bag high into a tree in the yard across from Emily's house. The other kids cheered and laughed.

Kristy smiled at Emily and Angela. "See you tomorrow!" she said.

And just like that, it was over. Angela and Emily watched in silence as the others moved off, laughing and congratulating one another.

In the living room, Hilary was oblivious to it all, deftly handling seven text conversations at once.

Up in Emily's bedroom, Dougie was as happy as could be. The game was the most realistic he had ever played—he almost felt as if he could reach out and touch the little characters who were scurrying around, thumping one another. Ugglins and Gugglins, they were called. He played and played, oblivious to his surroundings, so absorbed in the game that he barely noticed when he was . . . literally absorbed in the game.

"Ow," said Emily.

"Sorry," said Angela, who had one foot on Emily's head. She reached up to grab hold of a branch and then pulled herself awkwardly up into the tree.

"I'm so angry at them," said Emily, as she watched Angela climb higher toward the branch where the bag was dangling.

"I'm not," said Angela. "I mean, I guess I am, but who cares about them. But you know what's weird?"

"The fact that Kristy Meyer is so horrible for no reason? And also, *everything* that's happened over the past week?"

"Well, yeah, but about what just happened now."

Angela stepped onto another branch. Twigs rained down near Emily.

"It's like they weren't even thinking," said Angela. "Like they weren't even in control."

"They weren't. It was Kristy," said Emily. "Kristy's the ringleader. She made them do it."

"I guess," said Angela. She reached the desired branch and gave it a hard shake, and then another. The bag came loose and Emily caught it as it descended, more twigs and leaves falling around her. A few moments later Angela dropped down from the lowest branch and dusted herself off.

"What?" she said to Emily. "What are you thinking about?"

"Not sure," said Emily. There was something about what Angela had said that made her uneasy. Something about the look in Kristy's eyes. As if . . . as if someone else had been looking out through them. "You're right. It was like they weren't thinking for themselves," she said. "I'd never do it, but in the middle of it all, I had half a mind to get the Stone and . . ." She trailed off.

"What?" said Angela.

"The Stone," said Emily. "The Stone!" She turned and ran toward her house. "Come on!"

The first thing Emily saw when she and Angela burst into her room was the Stone lying on the floor. It was glowing. Emily snatched it up.

What she saw made her whole body go cold.

"Oh, no," she whispered.

CHAPTER
TWELVE

D ougie!" Emily said as loudly as she dared, holding the Stone up to her mouth. "Dougie!"

"What's going on?" said Angela.

"It's Dougie. My little brother. He's in here!" Emily said, pointing at the Stone. "It's like he got sucked into a game!"

Emily had summoned Gorgo almost immediately. Now he leaned in for a closer look. "Yep, that looks like him," he said.

The game appeared to still be in progress. The characters were all very small, but there could be no doubt: Dougie was in there, seated on a throne on top of a castle, apparently directing a battle.

"Oh, Dougie, you fool! He's always wanting to play games on my parents' phones. He must have somehow found this game, and . . ."

"Somehow?" said Angela. "You think this was an accident?"

"You're right. They must have done this. That family."

Their gazes met.

"All that with Kristy, it was just a distraction," said Angela. "So you'd go outside and be separated from the Stone."

"They're trying to get Dougie," said Emily.

"To get to you," finished Angela.

"I have to get him out of there!"

"Why?" said Gorgo. "Look at the points he's racking up! That has *got* to be a high score!"

The girls glared at him.

"Oh, c'mon, I'm just trying to lighten the mood!" he said. "But seriously, check out that score . . ."

Just then, the game quit, the placid window of the Stone returning.

"No!" Emily started to cry. "It's my fault!" she said between sobs. "It's all my fault! What am I going to do?"

Angela did her best to console her. Gorgo looked extremely uncomfortable. Then suddenly Emily stopped crying and seemed to be staring at nothing.

"What?" said Angela.

"If I can't get him out, I'm going to go get him."

"You know it's a trap," said Angela.

"I'm still going to go get him."

"I'm not sure you're going to be able to," said Gorgo.

Emily looked at him.

"You mean 'we,'" she said.

"Oh, no," he said.

"Oh, yes," she said. "You're coming with."

Turning her attention to the Stone, Emily muttered something to herself and then jabbed her finger at the magical device.

To Angela it appeared that Emily was just touching the smooth surface of the Stone. Then Angela watched in fascination as Emily placed the Stone on her night-stand and, with a very concentrated expression on her face, began moving her fingers in complex patterns— sometimes as if she were putting a finger on an invisible point in space, sometimes as though she were stretching taffy, sometimes as if she were weaving an unseen cat's cradle in midair. All the while she muttered and nodded to herself.

"What's she doing?" whispered Angela.

"Shh. She's mapping," said Gorgo. "Finding a route."

She was. Floating in front of Emily was a dazzling, luminous web of points and lines that stretched and changed as she moved them around. She didn't understand the map, exactly—she just *knew*, somehow, that she was seeing the infinitely complex connections between different worlds and realms and universes, seeing how some locations were apparently very distant but could be reached directly, while other, closer realms might require several steps to get there.

Sometimes her attention would waver and the whole thing would go hazy or start to fade.

Intention, Emily thought. *Concentrate on what you require, and let the Stone do the work.*

There! That's where Dougie was: a tiny glowing spot. And there, that nauseous green blob up here, that was where the Venomüches were. Of course—by following the interwoven lines, she could see why the Venomüches needed to first trap Dougie at an intermediate stop, because there was no direct route.

Angela watched Emily wave her hands as if clearing smoke, then snatch up the Stone again and peer intently at the screen. She jabbed the Stone with a finger again, put it down, and now started to make vertical motions with her hands as if she were dog-paddling, with the occasional sideways swipe.

"What's she doing now?"

"Arranging the travel," said Gorgo. "Hey, look, there's a deal on beach trips to Lankhmargh! Okay, okay, I'll be quiet."

Emily stopped the waving and swiping motions and seemed to be examining her handiwork.

"Three hundred TCs? Three hundred TwitCoins?" said Emily.

"What?" said Angela.

"That's how much it will cost to travel to where Dougie is and get him back," said Emily. "Three hundred TCs."

"Three hundred TwitCoins is a pretty good deal," said Gorgo.

"It doesn't matter how good a deal it is! It's three hundred TwitCoins more than I have!" said Emily.

"Oh, that *is* a problem," said Gorgo.

"Gorgo, where would I get TwitCoins?"

"Well . . ." said Gorgo, then cut himself off. He grimaced, squirming uncomfortably.

"Well what?"

"I . . ."

"Spit it out, Gorgo."

"I have some TwitCoins."

"So give them to me!"

"It's not that easy!"

"You have to obey me, Gorgo. I'm not *stealing* the money. I'll pay you back, somehow. What's the problem?"

"They're in my pigggy bank."

"Pig-iggy bank?" said Angela. "You mean 'piggy bank'?"

"No, I think he means 'pig-iggy bank,'" said Emily. "Is a pigggy bank to a piggy bank as a dogg is to a dog?"

"Yep. It's like a piggy bank, but it's a lot harder to get your money out."

"Why?"

"Because a pigggy bank will fight back."

"Wait," said Angela. "What's a dogg?"

"Like a doggg, but not as bad," said Gorgo.

"Thanks, that's helpful," said Angela.

"Gorgo, this is an emergency," said Emily.

"Okay, okay. But the real problem isn't that the TwitCoins are in my pigggy bank. The real problem is, my pigggy bank is at home."

"So let's go!"

He grimaced.

"What? How much does it cost to get there?"

"Oh, getting there is free. Getting *out* is the problem. And I don't think you'll find it a very pleasant place to visit."

"We have to risk it," Emily said, then looked at the

clock. "Four thirty. My mom will be home in an hour."

"Emily," said Angela, "what if it takes you longer? Or what if you go, and it's fast, but time moves differently in those other places? That's what the user's manual said. What if you're gone for a long time? Your parents will *freak*."

"You're right," said Emily. "It could be a day, or a week, or who knows how long!" She grabbed the Stone again and furrowed her brow in concentration, focusing her intention on *How do I keep people from knowing that Dougie and I are gone?*

A minute later she gasped. "It's me!"

"What?" said Angela.

"I'm waving at myself!" said Emily. And she was. Or at least, a miniature icon of herself was waving at her. Gorgo leaned over and looked.

"i-I?" he said. "That's what the apth is called?"

"Aye-aye?" said Angela.

"i-I, like the letters," corrected Emily. "It says it stands for 'imitation-I.' Hold on. Let me read the scroll. 'Looking to step out for a bit but can't get away? Why not leave yourself at home when you leave home?'"

She quickly read the instructions to Gorgo and Angela. *First*, it said, *build life-size mud statues of up to three people . . .*

"That's a lot of mud," said Gorgo.

"Yes. Where am I going to get that much?"

Angela was looking out the window.

"What?" said Emily. "What is it?"

"I think," said Angela, "I might have a suggestion."

Emily and Gorgo crowded next to her at the window to see what she was looking at: Mr. Petersen's garden, with its mounds of fresh black dirt.

"But he'll see us," said Emily.

"Leave that part to me," said Angela.

A few minutes later Mr. Petersen's doorbell rang. When he opened the front door, a girl he vaguely recognized was standing there.

"Hello, Mr. Petersen," said the girl. "My name is Angela Rodriguez, and I'd like to interview you for the Clearview school newspaper."

"Oh. Um . . . does it have to be now?"

"Yep," said Angela, flipping open her memo pad and readying her pen, "it sure does."

"I need more mud," said Emily urgently. "No, point the hose at the dirt, not at me!"

"Sorry," said Gorgo, and redirected the stream of water onto the dirt.

As Angela was conducting her interview with Mr. Petersen, Emily was working as quickly as she could, sculpting two life-size but very rough human figures with mud from Mr. Petersen's backyard garden. One of the figures was her height. The other was Dougie's.

The garden was next to a small shed toward the rear portion of the yard. Emily figured—well, hoped, really—that the shed, and the trees and fence ringing the yard, would block the other neighbors' view of what she was doing. But if Mr. Petersen happened to look out his back window, they were sunk. Which was why Angela was at his front door, doing her best to keep him busy.

The mud was staying together surprisingly well, as if the apth was already affecting it, but now Emily was running out of sculpting materials.

"You better hurry," said Gorgo.

"I know, I know!" said Emily. "Make more mud!"

In the front, Mr. Petersen was warming to the whole interview process, answering question after question. Angela asked him about his career path, favorite book, favorite food, favorite song . . .

"What about your advice to kids who want to become teachers?" she said. "Could you share some of your wisdom and insights?" She was trying to look as eager and attentive as possible while also being desperate to know what was going on out back. But the distraction was working, she thought. It was working!

"I'm glad you asked. First off, being a teacher is a calling, a sacred calling."

"Mm-hmm. Let me write that down. 'Sacred . . . calling.'"

"Exactly. A person should ask themselves—hold on a moment. I believe that's my house phone ringing."

"I don't think it is," said Angela.

"No, I'm pretty certain that's the phone."

"Well, they'll leave a message, won't they?"

"I should answer it—I'm waiting for the insurance company to contact me about my car."

"But—"

"Excuse me for a moment."

"Wait! I'm not done with the interview! Mr. Petersen! Come back!"

CHAPTER
THIRTEEN

E mily had two completed figures standing side by side. On the head of the smaller statue, she stuck one of Dougie's hairs that she had found on his pillow, then plucked one of her own hairs and placed it on the larger statue.

"What do you do next?" asked Gorgo.

"This," she said, and gently blew on each of them.

"Now, *that* is impressive," said Gorgo.

Emily stared at herself. And at her brother. They stared back at her. iEmily was dressed exactly like the real Emily. iDougie was dressed in the clothes he had been wearing when he disappeared.

"This is amazing," she said.

"And really, really creepy," said Gorgo.

"Can you speak?" said Emily to herself and iDougie.

"Yes," they both said at the same time.

"What is your name?" she said to iEmily.

"My name is Emily Edelman," iEmily responded. Her delivery was a bit flat and wooden, but her voice sounded exactly like the real Emily's.

"This is *perfect*," said Emily.

"You guys!" It was Angela, running to them from the side of the house. "Mr. Petersen went back inside! He—eeek!" she said, as iDougie and iEmily turned to look at her. "This is so freaky."

"Yes. I find it unnatural and disturbing," said Gorgo.

"Have you ever looked in a mirror?" said Emily.

"I've tried, but they generally crack," said Gorgo.

"I think you'd better hurry," said Angela. "Mr. Petersen got a phone call. He went back inside. He could be watching us right now!"

Mr. Petersen was talking on the phone with an insurance adjuster named Truly Wilshire.

"What a lovely name!" he said.

"Oh, thank you," she said, and laughed warmly.

Mr. Petersen was standing at the rear of his house. Luckily his back was to the window, because clearly visible behind him was his garden, and clearly visible in his garden were Angela, Dougie, Emily, *another* Emily, and a very large demonlike creature.

Mr. Petersen was having an absolutely delightful conversation with Ms. Wilshire. They started by talking about the strange occurrence with his car but soon wandered to other topics. "What?" he said. "You grew up in Minneapolis? Me too!"

As they talked and laughed and laughed and talked, a warm glow filled Mr. Petersen. He was, he realized, developing a crush on Ms. Wilshire. What a wonderful thing after all the strange events of the past few days! He pivoted around on his feet until he was facing the window and the backyard. Then his smile faded.

"Hello?" said Truly after she'd been talking for a bit with no response. "Hello? Evan? Mr. Petersen? Are you there?"

Mr. Petersen had forgotten about the phone. He had forgotten about Truly Wilshire. Instead he was gaping slack-jawed at what was happening in his backyard.

Emily was talking to Dougie and Angela. Also, Emily apparently had a twin, which Mr. Petersen hadn't known. But strangest of all was the man in a giant monster suit.

No, hold on, wait: the strangest part was the massive

doors that suddenly materialized out of nowhere. They looked like the twin doors of an elevator, but they were carved from rough stone. The doors parted, also like elevator doors, revealing an ornate interior lit with sconces. One of the Emilys exchanged a few words and a hug with Angela, and then she and the man in the monster suit went into the elevator—that's the only way Mr. Petersen could think of the strange doors—and then the doors shut. And then the doors vanished. Then Angela led Dougie and Emily Number Two out of the yard.

"Evan? Are you there? Hello?"

"I have to . . . go," said Mr. Petersen, and hung up. Then he went upstairs and had a lie-down.

Dougie was having the time of his life. This was the best game *ever!* He was seated on a wooden throne on the ramparts of a castle with a grand view of the battlefield before him. This was more like it! As soon as he had realized where he was, a throng of little warriors had surrounded him, hopping up and down with excitement.

"You king! You command!"

They came up to only his hips. They were mostly helmet, with little arms and legs sticking out. They were armed with clubs.

"You strategy! You command!"

All he had to do, he realized, was point and say, "Ten archers! There!" or "Catapult! There!" or "Foot soldiers! Attack!" and his orders were instantly obeyed. Wait till he told his friends about this awesome game!

Emily wasn't sure what traveling between dimensions would be like. She certainly hadn't been expecting the stone doors to appear before her right there in the garden. When they did, a pleasant female voice said, "Destination?"

She glanced at Gorgo. He cleared his throat—then kept clearing his throat, a rumbling, gargling, hacking growl. Finally, he stopped.

"You through? Are you going to say the name of the destination?" said Emily.

"That *was* the name of the destination."

There was a faint *bong* sound, and the doors opened.

"Please step in and stand clear of the closing doors," said the voice.

Emily turned to Angela. Before Emily could say anything, Angela said, "Don't worry. I'm on it. Go!"

"Thank you," said Emily, and then impulsively gave her a hug. Then she and Gorgo stepped in and the doors slid shut.

They were in what looked like an elevator draped

in ancient tapestries. Sconces burned without smoke. There were low wooden benches along both side walls and wooden railings to hold on to. Gentle music played, the sort Emily associated with educational documentaries about medieval times.

"It's like a magical elevator," said Emily.

"Funny you should say that," said Gorgo, "because—"

"Wait. You're going to say it's called a Spellevator."

"Yes! How did you know!"

"Next stop, ARRGHAMAHAHHRRRRRCCCHA-ARRAGHACHHHH," said the Spellevator's female voice, repeating the disturbing phlegmy exclamation Gorgo had emitted earlier.

"I just want to tell you again," said Gorgo. "Where we're going . . . I don't think you'll find it exactly pleasant."

"Okay."

Emily had no sensation of movement, but there was another soft *bong* and the doors slid open again.

"Whoa," she said, her eyes wide.

"I warned you," said Gorgo.

CHAPTER
FOURTEEN

Well, Dougie, your table manners are certainly excellent tonight," said Mr. Edelman.

"Thank you," said iDougie, who carefully cut himself another piece of his meatloaf and used his fork, not his hand, to transport that piece to his mouth. Then he chewed with his mouth shut and didn't speak while doing so.

Mr. Edelman and Mrs. Edelman exchanged looks of pleasant surprise. Hilary, however, who barely ever paid attention to anyone in her family, was watching iDougie with undisguised wonder.

"Anyway, ha ha, as I was saying, we have a wonderful unit in science class about invertebrates and we've been collecting pond water and looking at various paramecia under the microscope and it's really fascinating, don't you think, Emily?" said Angela. She was speaking very quickly and very nervously, and had been for most of the dinner.

"Yes, I think it's fascinating," said iEmily in an agreeable if not exactly expressive fashion.

Right before Gorgo and the real Emily had boarded the Spellevator, Angela and Emily had had a rushed conversation: further instructions on how to manage iDougie and iEmily, some directives for iEmily, and exchanges of good luck. And then Emily had thought of something else: she did a quick spell with an apth and handed Angela a stone from the garden.

"Here—it's sort of like a deputy Stone, for communication only. I should be able to call you on it and give you an update."

"Got it."

After they left, Angela had led iEmily and iDougie back to their home, the two of them following her obediently. Hilary didn't even look up from her screen when the three of them came in through the back door of the house.

Angela wasn't sure what to do—could she just leave the imitation Emily and Dougie and go home? They seemed so passive. They looked and sounded exactly like the real thing, and they would answer her questions when she spoke to them, but they were still somehow . . . off. They reminded Angela of cows

—content to sort of stand there, just existing, looking at nothing. Surely Emily's parents would notice something, wouldn't they?

Which is when Mrs. Edelman came home. She seemed so overjoyed that Emily had made a friend— "So nice to meet you!"—that Angela was worried that she was going to plant a kiss on her forehead. Then Mrs. Edelman had insisted Angela stay for dinner— "You just *have* to!"—and Angela realized maybe she had better do that. So she called her mom and told her about the invitation, and her mother seemed equally excited that *Angela* had a friend, and so Angela stayed for dinner.

At first everything was fine. Mostly Mrs. Edelman peppered Angela with questions—where do you live, how long have you lived here, do you like the school, and so on—and Angela was happy to keep talking. Both parents seemed entertained with their chatty, intelligent dinner guest and mostly unaware that their two younger children were acting a bit strange—which made sense to Angela, because she knew that most parents did a great job of *pretending* to pay attention to their kids without actually doing so.

The problem was Hilary. After they sat down to eat, Angela noticed that Hilary was glancing more and more often at iEmily and iDougie, her expression growing increasingly suspicious with each passing minute, and so Angela had started speaking faster and faster for longer and longer periods of time. Now, though, she had to take a breath, and as she did so, Hilary jumped in.

"Dougie, are you sick or something?" she asked.

"No," said iDougie. "Could you please pass the milk?"

Both parents gaped. Dougie had said "please"!

"Of course!" said Mr. Edelman, happily. Another glance at his wife—*Isn't this a wonderful development?*

"Dad," said Hilary, "there's something wrong with him!"

Angela began to sweat.

"Hilary!" said Mrs. Edelman. "Just because he's behaving like a grownup at the table—we are *so proud of you*, Dougie!—doesn't mean there's something wrong with him!"

"He's acting totally weird!" insisted Hilary. "And so are you!" she said to iEmily. "What is wrong with you? Why are you acting all uppity and brand-new?"

"I *am* brand-new," said iEmily. "I was just created an hour ago from—"

"Anyway," Angela jumped in with her desperately

cheerful tone, "Emily and I are *really* enjoying history class because we're studying the Tudor period in England, right, Emily? Right? Right? Right?"

"Right," said iEmily.

"I'm telling you, this is weird," said Hilary to her parents. "You don't think this is weird?"

"It's 'weird' that Dougie is behaving so nicely—*so* nicely, Dougie—and that Emily is enjoying her schoolwork?" said Mrs. Edelman.

"She really is," said Angela. "Like math class! What fun! Right, Emily?"

"Yes, lots of fun," said iEmily.

"You *hate* math!" said Hilary.

"It's so fun," said Angela.

"Fun," echoed iEmily.

"Okay, I think something *really strange* is—"

"Is everyone finished eating?" said Angela. "Maybe Dougie and iEmily—I mean, I *and* Emily—can all clear the table and wash the dishes!" She leaped up. iEmily and iDougie rose and started to help her. The parents beamed.

"This is extraordinary!" said Mr. Edelman.

Hilary had the stunned expression of someone watching an elephant break dance.

"Mom, Dad," she said, "don't you think that—"

"Don't just sit there, Hilary," said Mrs. Edelman. "Help them!"

So Hilary, her expression still incredulous, helped them clear the table.

"What are you doing?" she hissed at iEmily.

"I am now preparing to rinse this plate and put it in the—"

"Yes, yes, I *get* that, but what are you *doing*?"

"I am now rinsing the plate as I stated I would."

Angela took the opportunity to lean close to iDougie and whisper, "You should go get ready for bed and then go to sleep," and iDougie placidly announced that he was going to do just that.

Mr. Edelman and Mrs. Edelman followed him with their gazes as he left the room.

"He's like a changed person!" said Mr. Edelman.

"It's incredible!"

"It's bizarre!" said Hilary to them. "What are you up to?" she whispered at iEmily. "Are you and Dougie trying to make me look bad?"

"Your makeup is making you look bad," said iEmily. "You're wearing too much of it."

"Mom!"

"Okaaay!" said Angela. "Emily and I are going upstairs so she can help me with my homework because I need help with it and she's really smart and can help me with my homework, which I need help with. The homework. Right, Emily?"

"Right," said iEmily, and the two of them went upstairs.

"There is something definitely wrong with Dougie and Emily," said Hilary. "And that Angela girl is really weird!"

"Oh, Hilary," said Mrs. Edelman. "You should be happy that Dougie is behaving better and that Emily has a friend. And don't you have homework of your own to do?"

So Hilary went to do her homework, muttering the whole time. *Something weird is going on,* she thought, *and I'm going to figure out what it is.*

The heat was overwhelming. And the noise, an endless wailing and keening and moaning. And the sights — Emily had seen such things in horrifying paintings made by crazy artists in the Middle Ages. She tried to distract herself by identifying the stony landscape. Volcanic, she guessed.

"It's kind of nice to be home. Oh, look, there's Schmahoitchimet!" said Gorgo cheerfully, waving. "And

Zzaxtzl! And look, the old ice cream shop!" He glanced at Emily, and his expression changed. "Your skin is not supposed to be green, right?" he said.

"No," said Emily in a queasy voice.

"Why don't you close your eyes. I'll lead you."

"That sounds like a great idea."

She kept her eyes clamped tightly shut as Gorgo led her along by the hand. The horrific noises never ceased. Somehow hearing them without seeing what created them was almost worse.

Underneath her, the ground was rocky and uneven and it was difficult to walk without stumbling. They seemed to be heading gradually downhill, the heat growing even more intense as they did.

"Is this place . . . is it . . . you know," said Emily.

"Ah," said Gorgo. "Is it *h-e*-double-toothpicks? No, not in the way that your people might think of it. That said, as far as a human might be concerned, for all intents and purposes, it . . ."

"Is," Emily finished for him.

"Right."

She could feel him slowing, then coming to a stop.

"Okay," he said. "We're home. Here." Emily felt Gorgo's massive hands on her shoulders as he rotated her a quarter turn to her left. "My house is right in front of you. You can open your eyes. But I'll warn you again: what you see might shock you."

Steeling herself mentally, she cautiously opened her eyelids.

"Oh my goodness!"

"I told you," he said.

The narrow path they had followed had taken them to an isolated outcropping. All around her were distant mountains. The glowing red sky was matched by the glowing red of whatever was in the valleys far below them—lava flows? Right in front of them was Gorgo's home. It was not at all what she had been expecting.

"Is that a white picket fence?" said Emily.

"Sure is. Shall we go in?"

The house was a tidy little two-story home with white siding and a gray shingled roof. Well, not *little*—it was scaled to fit a creature of Gorgo's size. Otherwise it looked like any number of suburban homes that Emily had seen. Surrounding it was the white picket fence. There was a nicely tended lawn and a flower bed.

"She's very house-proud, my mom," explained Gorgo.

"You have a mom?"

"Of course!"

They walked along the path to the front entrance.

Gorgo reached for the handle to the screen door, then paused.

"You'll be safe," he said. Then thought a moment and added, ". . . ish. But my family . . ."

"You have a *family?*"

"Of course. My mom and three older brothers." He sighed. "The thing is . . . they can be *difficult.*"

Then he opened the screen door and the inner solid door and said, "Hello? I'm home."

It didn't take long for Emily to get a small sense of what Gorgo had meant by "difficult."

His apron-clad mother met him at the door, hugging him and pinching his cheeks and generally fussing over him, saying, "My baby's back! My widdle Gorgi is back!"

"Ma . . ." mumbled Gorgo. "C'mon . . ."

"What wonderful timing! I was just making shrapnel pie!"

Only then did she notice Emily.

"And who is *this* adorable little snack?" she said.

"This is Emily. Emily, this is my mother," said Gorgo. Emily noted that he was employing the same closed-mouth mumble she used when she had to introduce someone to her embarrassing parents.

"Oh, how lovely!" said his mother. The family

resemblance, Emily noted, was remarkable. In fact, his mother looked exactly like Gorgo, except with gray curly hair and a housedress and reading glasses. "Will we be having her for tea?"

"Not in the way you're thinking, Ma," said Gorgo.

"Pity. Well, come on back, the both of you," she said with a warm, maternal smile. "And WIPE YOUR FEET FIRST!!!" she bellowed suddenly, flames spurting from her mouth and ears. Emily jumped in fearful surprise and instantly began scraping her feet on the entryway mat with desperate enthusiasm. "Wonderful!" said Gorgo's mother with another smile. "Right this way!"

It wasn't until they were ushered into the kitchen that Emily *really* understood what "difficult" had meant.

"Ooh, look who it is! The runt is back!" roared a gigantic demon who had to be Gorgo's oldest brother.

"It's widdle Gorgi-Porgi!" roared another.

"The shrimp has returned!" roared the third.

Everything in the kitchen looked like what one would expect in the tidy white house. Just like the house itself, the furnishings were scaled up to fit creatures who were much larger than human beings.

The three brothers were seated around a massive circular table, plates of scones and dainty cups of tea in front of them. And they were right: compared to them, the massive Gorgo looked like a runty widdle shrimp.

"And who's this?" asked the biggest one, pointing to Emily. "Honey."

For a moment Emily wasn't sure if he was calling her honey or calling his mother honey — and then saw that he was gesturing with one claw for his middle brother to pass him a jar of honey. "She looks like she'll taste great dipped in this," said the biggest brother.

"No one is touching her!" said Gorgo.

"Ooh! No one's touching her! Widdle shrimpy Gorgo says so!" The brothers waved their claws and widened their eyes in mock fear, giggling and guffawing.

"This is Emily," said Gorgo. "Emily, these are . . . my brothers. Such as they are."

"Where you been, brother?" asked the middle one. "How was the *rock* show?" he said, then laughed uproariously at his own joke, high-fiving the others. "Get it? The *rock* show?"

"Yeah!" said the third. "What happened? Get stuck between a rock and, I don't know, a rock?"

More rough laughter. "What was it," said the oldest, "a *rock* concert? HA HA HA HA!"

Gorgo rolled his eyes. Emily heard him mutter, "And they wonder why I never wrote . . ."

Their mother was at the counter, kneading some sort of dough. Emily wasn't sure, but she thought she heard the dough saying, "Ouch! Ooh! Ouch!" It was hard to tell over all the guffawing.

"Boys, be nice to your baby brother," said their mother indulgently. "BAMPILANGAYANGCHICHAR-ONIMUS, YOU GET YOUR ELBOWS OFF THE TABLE *RIGHT NOW!!!*"

"Sorry, Mum," said the eldest, as Emily tried to get her heart to stop thumping.

"Gorgi, have you been eating enough? You look terrible," said his mother. The brothers sniggered.

"Ma, please, I'm not a baby . . ."

"Who gets himself wizarded into a rock?" said the youngest. "'Ooh, I'm just going to stop and help this lovely maiden. I sure hope a wizard doesn't come along and trap me in a rock for an eternity.'"

"HA HA HA HA!!" they all laughed.

"I was not going to *help* her, I was going to *eat* her!" said Gorgo. He looked pleadingly at Emily. "I was!" he insisted. "I was planning to eat her, and then suddenly there's this wizard, and he's all, like, 'Begone, foul creature . . .'"

"Hey, Gorgo," said the middle one, "and then what happened? You had to get freed by a *little girl!*"

"Gorgo has to serve a little girl! HAR HAR HAR!!!"

"Yeah, what's she making you do, play with dolls? HAR HAR HAR!!!"

"All right, I've had enough of this," said Gorgo. He turned to Emily. "I have to go up to my old room to deal with my pigggy bank."

"I'll come with you."

"No, just stay here. You'll be safe."

They both glanced at the three cackling brothers.

". . . ish," said Emily.

"Well, safer than if you had to deal with the pigggy bank." Gorgo pointed a claw at his brothers. "I'm going upstairs now. You know the rules: you can't even touch her." He marched over to the long kitchen counter and opened the last drawer, from which he pulled out a huge hammer.

"What are you doing?" asked the middle brother.

"None of your business." As Gorgo passed by Emily, he said, "I'll be back soon. I'd suggest not eating anything."

CHAPTER
FIFTEEN

As was previously stated, time moves differently for different realms. Not just in easy ratios, either, such as one day being equal to two weeks, and so on. More like, one hour might equal a day, but then the very *next* hour might equal just five minutes, and then the *next* might equal half a day . . . which is a long-winded way of explaining that right now it was the next day in Clearview. And there were problems.

Angela was sitting in her civics class, watching with rising apprehension as Mrs. Henkins got more and more annoyed. The source of her annoyance: each time she started talking to the class, there would be a *scritch-scratch-scribble* noise that would end as soon as she turned from the blackboard to see who was responsible for it.

Angela's spot was the last one in the last row in the back corner. Emily—iEmily, that is—was seated across the room toward the front, so Angela didn't have a good view of her. But she could tell that was where the scritch-scratch-scribbling was coming from and was just now remembering one of real Emily's final instructions to iEmily: *Pay attention and take notes on everything the teachers say.*

"So," Mrs. Henkins said, "the judicial branch of the government . . ." As she spoke, the scribbling started again. There were some scattered giggles. The teacher jerked her head around. The scratching and giggling stopped. She faced the blackboard and started talking again.

"The judicial branch of the government includes the —okay, who is doing that!!"

She glared at the classroom. More poorly stifled giggles.

"Sorry, Mrs. Henkins," said Angela. "I'm just taking some notes."

"You were doing that?"

"Yes, ma'am."

"Mrs. Henkins, it wasn't her," said Kristy. "It was Emily." She twisted around to smile poisonously at Angela.

"Mrs. Henkins," said Angela, "it *was* me taking notes. I just want to make sure I don't miss anything!"

Angela darted a glare at Kristy.

"Okay, fine. I don't care who it is," said Mrs. Henkins. "Just please do it more . . ." She hesitated. "Do it more . . ." She hesitated again. "Qui . . . et . . . ly."

Mrs. Henkins was speaking in that start-stop manner because she kept getting distracted by iEmily, who was staring back at her intently, pencil poised above her notebook.

"I didn't mean to be a nuisance!" said Angela from the back of the room, desperate to divert Mrs. Henkins's attention.

"You're being a nuisance right now, Angela," said Mrs. Henkins. She was still watching iEmily, because the instant the teacher started to talk, iEmily started writing in her notebook at an impossible speed.

"Um, Mrs. Henkins?" said Angela.

Mrs. Henkins held up a hand. "Hold on a moment," she said.

"I just . . ."

"Be quiet!"

Scribble scribble.

"Emily," said Mrs. Henkins, "what are you" — *scribble*

scribble scribble — "doing? Are you just doodling" — *scribble scribble* — "in your notebook?"

"I'm taking notes, Mrs. Henkins," said iEmily.

More giggles throughout the classroom.

Mrs. Henkins walked over to iEmily's desk and looked down at the notebook. Her eyes widened. The pages were entirely covered with perfect handwriting.

Today we'll be discussing the tripartite structure of our government. Tripartite means ... Where is the chalk ... Hold on ... There we go. Tripartite means "three parts." Let me put that on the board.

That was just a small portion of the paragraphs and paragraphs of notes. As if iEmily had transcribed every single word Mrs. Henkins had said.

"Emily, are you writing down every single word . . ." The teacher stopped talking, because Emily was doing exactly that, writing each word as fast as Mrs. Henkins could speak, her pencil a blur. ". . . I say?" she finished.

Scribble scribble.

"Oh, dear," said Mrs. Henkins.

iEmily dutifully wrote *that* down, too.

. . . .

Meanwhile, in Dougie's classroom in the lower school at Clearview School, Dougie was behaving perfectly. He did not yell. He did not run. He did not throw anything. Another student made a large tower out of blocks and Dougie did not knock it down.

Dougie's teacher found this worrisome.

In the early afternoon, Mr. Edelman called his wife at work.

"Hi, honey. You know, I was thinking about what Hilary was saying last night, and then I got a call from Dougie's teacher—he wanted to know if Dougie was feeling okay. Said he was acting a bit weird. 'Off,' as he put it."

"Can I tell you something?" said Mrs. Edelman. "I just got off the phone with one of Emily's teachers, who said the same thing."

Just as time moves oddly between dimensions, it sometimes flows oddly *within* dimensions. For example, it was only three o'clock, but for Angela it seemed as though her first school day with iDougie and iEmily had lasted for several eternities.

That morning, she had appeared at the Edelmans' door before school. "Hi!" she said to Mrs. Edelman. "I was hoping maybe I could walk to school with Emily and Dougie."

"How wonderful!" said Mrs. Edelman.

So Angela had left the house with iEmily and iDougie, aware that Hilary was watching them go with a raised eyebrow.

Angela escorted the two clones to school. Before she sent iDougie off to his classroom—where he'd stay the whole day, because that's what they did in first grade—she'd said, "Behave today."

"Okay," he said.

Then Angela had done her best to watch over iEmily in the halls and in the classes that they shared, like the civics class with Mrs. Henkins earlier in the day. Wherever she went with iEmily, the other kids parted to let them pass, not even bothering to hide their stares.

Finally the day was over. Angela had picked up iDougie from his classroom and then waited with iEmily in the upper school until most of the kids had left. She was now walking with iEmily and iDougie down an empty hallway, heading toward a rear exit.

Angela didn't know how school would be tomorrow,

but she was grateful to have made it through today. All she had to do was—

"Hey, stupid!"

Angela looked up. Kristy had just rounded the corner and was blocking their path, her hands on her hips.

"Kristy, please, not now," said Angela.

"Oh, what's wrong, Alice? You scared?"

"My name is Angela. And yes, I'm scared, but not of you."

Kristy snorted. Then, "What are *you* looking at?" she said to iEmily.

"I'm looking at you," responded iEmily.

"Well, stop doing that."

"Okay," said iEmily, and diverted her gaze just slightly away from Kristy. iDougie stood silently next to his isister.

"What is wrong with you?" said Kristy.

"Kristy, please, you don't understand," said Angela.

"I don't understand? Why, do you think I'm stupid?"

"Kristy, we're just trying to—"

"What about you, Emily? Do you think I'm stupid?"

iEmily appeared to consider this.

"Possibly," she said.

"You know who's stupid?" spat Kristy. "You are. Stupid and ugly. You should pull your own head off."

"You mean, like this?" said iEmily.

Kristy's scream echoed down the school hallways.

"Oh, no," whispered Angela, looking down at Kristy's unconscious form. She turned to iEmily. "Oh, for goodness' sake! Put your head back on!"

Angela stayed with Kristy until she sat up woozily, shaking her head, and said, "What happened?"

"Nothing happened! It's fine it was all a dream you dreamed it it wasn't real you dreamed it bye!" babbled Angela as she fled down the hall with iEmily and iDougie in tow.

This was a disaster. What was going on with the real Emily? Would she ever call on the rock, which Angela was now carrying around everywhere? Would Emily ever come back? How long before iDougie and iEmily turned to mud again? Could things possibly get worse?

Which is what Angela was thinking just as she reached the Edelman front door and it opened from the inside and Hilary was standing right there, smiling.

"Hi there!" said Hilary.

"Uh . . . hi!"

"So glad you two are home," Hilary said to iDougie and iEmily, then grabbed them both by the arm and yanked them inside.

"Wait!" said Angela. "Can I come in?"

"Nope," said Hilary, and closed the door in Angela's face.

Oh, Emily, thought Angela. *Where are you?!*

CHAPTER
SIXTEEN

Where was Emily? She was still in the kitchen with Gorgo's mother and brothers. A moment ago, Gorgo had left the room. Emily could hear his footsteps climbing the stairs. The three brothers were giggling and saying things in low tones that made them giggle more. Emily could distinctly make out an occasional "Ooh!" and "Ouch!" from the dough that Gorgo's mom was kneading.

"Look at her," the eldest brother was saying. "What luck. She gets a demonic servant, and it turns out to be that pathetic idiot."

"Yeah, widdle runty stupid Gorgi."

From upstairs came a crashing sound, then the grunts and squeals of what Emily envisioned as a gigantic and very angry wild boar. More crashing. Gorgo yelling something that Emily guessed was a series of very bad words.

Squeals and grunts, the sound of glass breaking, some-thing wooden getting smashed.

The rest of the family seemed not to notice the ti-tanic struggle happening on the second floor.

"Can you imagine ending up with Gorgi as your de-monic servant?" one of the brothers was saying. "Awful. Pathetic. Makes me laugh."

"Completely agree."

"Absolutely."

Emily, to her surprise, found herself getting angry.

"Well, you know what?" she said to the brothers. They looked at her in surprise. "You think you're all such great catches? Forget it. I think *you're* pathetic. And I don't care how he got stuck in that rock. Maybe he *was* trying to help some maiden. Well, good for him. And maybe he'll end up eating me, but I have to say, I'd rather it be him than any of you jerks. At least he's good company, and helpful, and friendly in his own weird way. He's actually likable. There, I said it. I *like* him. Who would like you? Oh, and also? Your stupid jokes? They're *stupid*."

The three brothers blinked in bewildered silence at the small, brave girl in front of them. A little wisp of smoke rose from the head of the eldest brother. Their mother had stopped kneading and was staring at her.

Emily was aware that the sounds of struggle from upstairs had ended.

"Well, I never," said the mother.

The floor creaked. Emily looked over her shoulder. Gorgo came limping into the kitchen, trying to catch his breath. He looked somewhat beat up. But he was holding a large burlap sack in one hand.

"I . . ." he gasped, "got them."

He looked around, noting the tension in the room. "What happened here?"

"Your young friend was just giving us a lecture on civility," said his mother.

"I'm sorry, ma'am," said Emily. "I didn't intend to be rude, but they were being so mean."

"I understand, dearie," said Gorgo's mother. "That's very sweet of you to stick up for little Gorgo. NOW GET OUT OF MY HOUSE!!"

Emily shrieked and ducked a jet of flame.

"Is this okay?" asked iDougie.

Hilary surveyed his room. It had never been this clean.

"It's really good," she said, trying to control the shaking in her voice. "Great job."

The afternoon had started out as lots of fun. But the

fun had quickly faded away. Now Hilary was having one of the most disturbing, frightening days that she could remember.

Since last night's dinner she had been thinking of ways to figure out what was going on with Emily and Dougie. This whole goody-two-shoes thing they were doing—they were up to something, she was sure of it. *But what?*

Then she had made a decision: if they wanted to play that game, well, let them. *Let's see how far they'll go with it,* she had thought.

So after she'd slammed the door in the face of that weird Angela girl, Hilary had turned to iDougie and iEmily and said, "You guys want to hang out or something?"

"I have to do my homework," said iEmily flatly, and disappeared upstairs.

Perfect, thought Hilary. *I'll start with Dougie.*

"Dougie, do you want to play?" said Hilary.

It sounded strange coming out of her own mouth. She couldn't remember the last time she had asked to spend time with either of them. And she knew how the normal Dougie would respond: "Blech! No!"

But iDougie said, "Okay."

Excellent. He wanted to keep up the act. *And he's gonna pay for it,* thought Hilary.

"Great!" said Hilary. She already knew what she was going to suggest, the most absurd, ridiculous, sure-to-be-laughed-at proposal. "We're going to play dolls."

But iDougie didn't laugh. He didn't say "Blech!" He just said, "Okay."

So they played dolls.

At first, Hilary had been laughing inside. She knew that it must have been torture for him. But iDougie kept up the act, patiently playing dolls with her.

As they played, Hilary began to get annoyed. It's not like she particularly enjoyed playing with dolls—she was way too old for that. But she knew it must have been driving her brother crazy with boredom. *Surely he'll start complaining after a few minutes,* she thought, *or start throwing things.* But he didn't. And the longer they went on, the more irritated she became.

"Aren't you bored?" she asked him.

"No," he said.

Okay, fine, she thought. *We'll take it to the next level.*

"Dougie," she said, "this basement is a mess. Put all your toys into the toy chest."

Without a word of complaint, he stood up and began

to put the toys away. And that's when Hilary had begun to feel the first inklings of unease.

That unease intensified as she watched her little brother work, picking up each item diligently and without whining. The unease became concern when he finished the job, turned to her, and said, "What next?"

So she said, "Now go practice the piano," and he went and dutifully practiced the piano. The concern shifted to worry.

Then Hilary had said, "Okay, that's enough. Go clean your room."

"Okay."

The worry started to edge toward alarm.

This was not some trick. This was something else. There was something deeply, deeply wrong with Dougie.

"Now what?" said iDougie now. The room was perfect. He had *folded his clothes*. He had *made the bed*.

Hilary felt her alarm tipping very decidedly toward panic.

"Just . . . just stay here and play quietly," said Hilary.

"Okay," said iDougie.

Hilary, blinking back tears and trying not to hyperventilate, went to Emily's door and knocked on it.

"Yes?"

Hilary bit her fist, stifling a sob. Just "yes"? Not "I'm BUSY" or "Go AWAY"? *What was going on?!*

"Emily? Can I come in?"

"Yes."

iEmily was sitting at her desk. She turned when Hilary entered and regarded her with no expression.

"I'm going to tell you something," said Hilary, her voice quivering. "I want you to listen carefully to it."

"Okay," said iEmily.

"I have a friend named Alexis who likes this guy Henry, but Henry likes . . ."

Hilary continued to talk for nearly a minute, giving iEmily an extremely detailed update of her peer group's ever-evolving social landscape. During which time her sister did not squirm, roll her eyes, sigh, drum her fingers, shake her head, jiggle her feet, space out, or do *anything whatsoever to indicate boredom*. All she did was *listen*.

Hilary burst into tears. "What is *wrong* with you guys?!" she said, and fled into her own room and slammed the door, still weeping.

iEmily simply turned back to the desk and did what she had been doing before: sat there.

Hilary collapsed on her bed, head in her hands, and sobbed. She couldn't *stand* her brother and sister—really, not at all, not a bit. No way. Ask anyone.

But she really, really, *really* wanted them back. Because these people, she knew, were not the real thing.

The real Dougie was no longer having any fun either.

At first sitting on the throne and wearing the crown and overseeing the battlefield had been enjoyable. But then it became tiresome. The attacks by the Gugglins never stopped. They would pause, yes, but Dougie quickly learned that the combat was just like the fights in the games he played on the computer: if you defeated one wave of attackers, the next wave would be stronger and faster and better equipped, and the next wave yet more so, and so on and so on. And the waves looked as though they would keep coming forever.

"What now?" demanded the Ugglins. "What defense? What do?"

"Can't we take a break?" asked Dougie. "I'm tired!"

"No break! No stop!" said the Ugglins.

From the field of battle Dougie could hear the endless sounds of struggle: the clang of weapons on armor, roars, shouts of alarm and anger.

"I'm hungry," said Dougie.

"No eat!"

"The crown itches!"

"Keep crown!"

"I have to go to the bathroom!"

"No bathroom!"

"When can I stop?"

"Never stop! Never!"

CHAPTER
SEVENTEEN

Emily stumbled out onto Gorgo's front porch.

"Don't forget to write, dear," she heard Gorgo's mother say.

"Okay, Ma, I—" said Gorgo, but that's as far as he got before the door slammed shut violently.

Gorgo sighed and rubbed his face. "Sorry about all that in there," he said.

"No," said Emily, "I feel sorry for *you*."

Gorgo held up the burlap sack. "At least we got the TwitCoins," he said. He opened the sack, a faint glow emerging. Emily looked inside. The glow was coming from the coins themselves, which were the size of drink coasters and as thick as her pinkie. Despite that, there was something vaguely transparent about them, as if they couldn't make up their mind whether to exist or not.

"They're sort of spread around lots of dimensions at the same time," said Gorgo, noting her quizzical expression. "Anyhow, I think we'd better hurry. You have to get the coins into the Stone."

"Right," said Emily. She looked at the Stone. "Um . . . how do I do—"

Before she could finish, the Stone leaped from her hand directly into the burlap sack. "Whoa!"

Then Gorgo had to struggle to hold on to the sack as some sort of battle raged within it, coins clinking loudly, the sack heaving and bulging and leaping about as though an angry cat were chasing mice inside.

Then suddenly the bag went completely limp. Gorgo opened it and peered inside, snapping his head back just in time as the Stone leaped out and into Emily's hand. "Yikes!" she exclaimed.

Gorgo turned the bag inside out. It was completely empty.

"Well," he said, tossing the bag away, "I think you figured it out. Hurry up—get those tickets."

Thirty seconds of concentration and apth-ing later and she had. "There!" she said. "There's the Spellevator!"

But the doors weren't right in front of them. They

had instead appeared farther up the narrow path Emily and Gorgo had taken to get to Gorgo's house. "C'mon!" said Emily.

As they left Gorgo's yard and hurried along the path toward the doors, Emily was thankful she'd had her eyes closed the first time. The path was so very narrow that in some places it was no wider than a skateboard. On both sides sheer cliffs dropped down to flowing lava or depths hidden by roiling smoke. She couldn't for the life of her figure out how she and Gorgo had navigated the path the first time. And had it been so steep? In fact, it seemed to be getting steeper with each step she took. All the while she had a growing sense of certainty that time was running out, that Dougie would soon be beyond her reach—and that the Spellevator doors wouldn't wait for them much longer. She looked up from the path to check their progress and gasped.

"Gorgo," Emily said, out of breath, "it doesn't seem like the doors are getting any closer!"

"I told you," he said. "It's easy to get here. It's the leaving that's hard."

"We have to hurry!" She sped up her pace. She desperately wanted to run but didn't dare do so over the broken, treacherous ground, knowing that one misstep could send her plummeting over an edge. "Gorgo! Can't you grab me and jump there or something? Gorgo? Gorgo!"

But Gorgo didn't answer. Emily turned and looked at him. He was still walking along the path, but he seemed as if he was in the midst of a pleasant daydream, his expression serene and happy.

"Gorgo! Gorgo, what is wrong with you! Gorgo, you —EEEEE!" Emily shrieked as a hand clamped around her right ankle, then another, and another, forearms sprouting from the very ground itself, reaching for her legs, another hand now grabbing her other ankle.

"Let me go!" she screamed. "Let me go!" She kicked her feet, tearing her ankles from the grasping hands, but there were more, and then more. "Gorgo! Help me!" she screamed.

He looked at her with a dazed, goofy expression on his face. "What?" he said. "What's wrong?" *He's bewitched*, Emily realized, and knew at that moment that it was the toxic magic of this place trying to hold them both here, and in just a few more seconds the Spellevator doors were going to close and she'd be trapped forever.

It was dinnertime at the Edelmans'.

Mr. Edelman, Mrs. Edelman, and Hilary were

spending a lot of time glancing at iEmily and iDougie and then glancing at one another. Both of the younger children were once again eating with perfect manners. At no point did iDougie try to steal anything from iEmily's plate. Nor did iEmily reject her lima beans.

"Are you guys feeling all right?" said their father. He had asked this same question about five times already.

"Yes," they answered in unison.

More glances were exchanged.

"Okay. Well, Dougie, why don't you take your plate in, then go upstairs and start getting ready for bed."

Without a word, iDougie rose, took his plate to the sink, rinsed it, and placed it in the dishwasher. Then he disappeared upstairs.

Hilary leaned closer to her parents. "You see? You see what I've been telling you?"

She was close to tears. She and her parents now turned to look at iEmily. iEmily didn't seem to be looking at anything. She didn't seem to be unhappy. She just seemed to . . . be.

Her mother watched her younger daughter, her concern mounting.

"Emily," said her mother, "why don't you go outside and, I don't know, jump rope or something."

"Okay," said iEmily. She got up, took her jump rope off the hook by the door, and went outside.

"I'm going to check on Dougie," said Mr. Edelman, and went upstairs.

A few minutes later Mr. Edelman came downstairs with a worried expression on his face. He found his wife and Hilary standing by the front window, staring outside. They turned when he came into the room.

"What's wrong?" said Mrs. Edelman.

"It's Dougie."

"What's he doing?"

"I went up there, and he was brushing his teeth."

Mr. Edelman paused to let this sink in. This was the second night in a row Dougie had just brushed his teeth. Dougie did not usually just brush his teeth, at least not without several minutes of bargaining and threats and eventual yelling.

"What's that whistling noise?" asked Mr. Edelman.

"It's Emily," said Hilary. Then she burst into tears.

"What?" said Mr. Edelman.

Mrs. Edelman gestured to the window. Outside, iEmily was jumping rope. Very fast. Very, very fast. So fast that the jump rope was really just a blurry shell surrounding her. That's where the whistling noise was coming from. iEmily, however, did not seem to be exerting herself in the least.

"I wonder if the pediatrician's office has any availability tomorrow," said Mr. Edelman.

More and more hands were bursting forth from the rocky ground and grabbing Emily's legs, immobilizing her. "Let me go!" she screamed again, and slammed the Stone down onto the knuckles of one of the hands. It instantly released her and shriveled away into a blackened curl. She smashed at all the other hands with the Stone, each hand and forearm shriveling as she did so.

Up ahead the open doors of the Spellevator beckoned. They were only a short dash away. But even as Emily looked at them, the doors started to close.

"No!" she screamed, smashing at the final hand and starting to run. The doors were halfway closed when she reached them, and she leaped between them, holding them apart. They opened up again like elevator doors would but immediately started to close again, and this time kept closing when she pressed her hands against them.

"Gorgo!" Emily yelled. He was still about twenty yards away, his expression childlike and vacant. Emily pressed her back against one of the doors and her hands and feet against the other, struggling mightily against them, and still they were slowly inching closed. "Gorgo!" she screamed again. "Gorgo!" Nothing. "Gorgo, I command you to wake up!"

Nothing. Keeping one hand on the door, she held the Stone up, reaching out with her intention, and found and initiated an apth.

A giant hand bell materialized next to Gorgo's head and began ringing. He didn't notice.

"Something else!" said Emily.

The bell transformed into a gloved hand, a finger tapping him on the shoulder.

"No—more!" yelled Emily.

The hand seemed to hear her and began slapping Gorgo across the face. Nothing.

"More!"

The hand became a giant fish, also slapping him across the face.

"It's not working!"

The fish became a big wooden bucket, which wound up and dashed its watery contents in his face.

Gorgo shook his head, blinking and sputtering.

"Gorgo!"

Emily knew that she had just moments before the doors would overpower her and she'd be crushed to death.

"Gorgo! Over here!"

Gorgo finally seemed to come to full consciousness. Wiping his face, he looked around and saw her predicament. With one leap he sailed through the air and landed in front of the doors, grunting with effort as he spread them apart with his giant hands. Released from the doors' deadly grip, Emily fell to the floor inside the Spellevator and Gorgo squeezed in afterward, the doors crashing shut with a boom behind him.

"Why are you playing around?" he said. "We have things to do!"

CHAPTER
EiGHTEEN

Acrimina Venomüch was on a mission.

She moved with grace and elegance across the crowded ballroom, greeting old friends, smiling her dazzling smile, blowing kisses, pausing briefly to take the opportunity to slip poison into a one-time rival's champagne. She doubted it would kill her—the rival was too wily for that. But—*sigh*—one did what one could.

The ball was legendary. It was an annual event (not annual in Earth years; annual in the sense that . . . never mind. It's too hard to explain. It was annual). It was thrown by a very prominent and important family from one of the *best* universes. It was extravagantastical; it was grandeuropuluxurianificent. It was *fancy*.

The guests were also fancy. They were from many

times and places. Not all were evil, like the Venomüches. But there probably weren't a lot of attendees that you would call *good*.

Acrimina fairly floated through the bejeweled and lavishly appointed crowd. She caught a glimpse of her rival cleverly passing off the champagne glass to another guest, the rival's rival, and Acrimina sighed again. Who knew who would end up with it. But the guests at this event didn't get where they were by being easily duped into drinking poisoned champagne.

No matter. The attempt on her rival's life was a minor diversion, just something extra thrown in while Acrimina was here. She had another, far more important target this evening. And there he was. She put on her most charming smile.

"Ah, Baron von Varonbon!" she said.

"Archduchess!"

Cheeks were kissed. Chatting commenced. The elderly baron was portly and cheerful, his military uniform nearly invisible under the layers of medals he wore. They jiggled as he guffawed at Acrimina's lively wit. Her eyes sparkled. Occasionally she would reach out and brush his arm as they talked, the baron enchanted by the attention paid to him by such a beautiful, alluring specimen.

It was only later, after the party had ended, that he realized his priceless ceremonial dagger was no longer clipped to his belt, and he wondered what might have happened to it.

Dr. Harold Longmeer glanced through the window at his waiting room. Phew—only two more patients for the day, a boy who appeared to be around six years old and a girl around twelve. The office nurse had let him know that they were siblings. From this distance, sitting quietly next to their parents, they both appeared in fine physical shape.

He didn't know either of the children—in fact, he hadn't been a doctor very long and had just joined this practice a few weeks ago. Today had been the most unusual he'd had so far, with a visit from a girl named Kristy who had apparently fainted at school. "She kept repeating something about one of the students removing her own head!" the girl's mother had told him.

"I'm sure she'll be fine," he had told the mother. Some sort of benign juvenile fainting episode, he figured. Perhaps low blood sugar. The hallucination she reported didn't bother him much—people often had strange visions or dreams when they lost consciousness.

"Send the next patient in," he said to the nurse now. "Let's start with the boy."

"Well, now, young man," said Dr. Longmeer when iDougie entered the examination room. "Why don't you have a seat here on the table."

The boy complied.

"So, how do you feel? Good?"

"I don't."

"You don't feel good?"

"I don't feel," said the boy.

Huh, thought the doctor. "Okay. Well, let's check your pulse and take a quick listen to your heart."

About a minute later the doctor was in a state of barely controlled panic, having spent the previous sixty seconds trying in vain to find (a) a pulse, and (b) the sound of a heartbeat. Several minutes later his anxiety had increased even further, because he had now discovered that his patient had no reflexes, that his pupils didn't contract as they should when a bright light was shined at them, that he didn't seem to have lungs, and that he had a body temperature of 72 degrees, which was coincidentally where the thermostat was set. Meaning he was room temperature.

"How am I, Doctor?" asked iDougie in an expressionless voice.

"F-fine, fine," said Dr. Longmeer, his voice shaking. "Why don't I have a look at your sister."

Several minutes after *that*, when he had taken the same measurements on iEmily, Dr. Longmeer felt a strong need to hold on to the edge of the exam table, because it felt as though the universe were swinging about him in a very discomfiting manner.

"Emily," he said, his own voice coming from what seemed like a long way away, "may I ask you a question?"

"Yes, Doctor."

"Can you," began the doctor, not believing he was about to ask this of a patient, "remove your own head?"

About fifteen seconds later, Mr. Edelman and Mrs. Edelman saw the doctor emerge into the waiting room and walk with great purpose toward the exit, his eyes focused intently on the floor in front of him. "A specialist. Need a specialist," he was muttering repeatedly.

"Dr. Longmeer?" said Mr. Edelman. "Dr. Longmeer!"

The doctor seemed to take notice of them for the first time.

"How was the examination? Is everything okay?"

"Need a specialist," repeated the doctor.

"The children need a specialist?" said Mrs. Edelman, alarmed.

Dr. Longmeer seemed confused for a moment. "What? Oh. The children. Yes. I suppose they do. I was referring to myself."

With that, he turned and walked out the front door.

"Here it is," said Acrimina, displaying the dagger to Maligno Sr. He took it from her reverently and carefully drew the weapon from its jewel-encrusted scabbard. The blade gleamed in the greenish light from the flames in the skull fireplace.

"The blade looks like opal," he said.

"It's a type of pearl, darling."

"It seems to be glowing."

"It's *special* pearl, darling."

Many materials can be used to make an enchanted blade. Dragon teeth are popular. Hydra scales. Griffin claws. Iron from meteorites. But this particular blade was made from the heart of a pearl. A large pearl. One that, if whole, would be about the size of a beach ball. A pearl created by a mollusk the size of a city block.

"It's from a dire lava clam," said Acrimina. "From deep inside the lower depths."

"Of course, of course," said Maligno Sr., admiring the dagger. "And it will do the job?"

"It's the only blade that can. It will sever the magic link that binds the demon to the girl. And once he's free . . ."

"Yes," said Maligno, and smiled. "I wonder if he'll need salt and pepper."

CHAPTER
NINETEEN

The Spellevator bucked and rattled like a jet plane in heavy turbulence.

"Gorgo, what's going on?" said Emily. "Why is it taking so long?"

"I think it's them. You know who. I think they're somehow trying to stop you."

The Spellevator jerked again and would have sent Emily sprawling if Gorgo hadn't caught her.

"Are you okay?" he said.

"Are you?"

"I sometimes get a little motion sick," he said.

"Are you gonna throw up?"

"I hope not," he said.

Emily tried not to think about what it would be like if a fire-breathing creature Gorgo's size got sick.

"Me too," she said.

Another big bump, then another, and another, until the turbulence was so intense that even Gorgo struggled to hold on. It was all Emily could do to keep from crying out in terror.

When it seemed as if the tumult had gone on forever and would go on forevermore, Gorgo said, "I think . . . I think it's getting better. I think we're nearly there."

And indeed the bumps were lessening, and then stopped altogether.

"We're here," said Gorgo. "It should be a lot better from here on out."

Then the doors opened behind him to reveal a massive boulder flying directly at them.

"Look out!" said Emily, and dived to the floor.

Gorgo spun an instant before the impact and punched the boulder away, shattering it. Smaller rocks and dust rained down on Emily.

"Ha!" said Gorgo. He turned back to her, grinning. "Pretty good, right?"

"Gorgo!" she said.

"Huh?"

CRACK! Another flying boulder shattered on the back of his head. More rocks and dust covered Emily.

"ARGH!" Gorgo clutched at his skull. "That *does* it!"

Flames jetted from his skin. He dashed out of the Spellevator and onto what Emily now realized was a field of battle, swatting at miniature warriors with abandon. "Gorgo!" she shouted, and ran out of the Spellevator, the doors closing behind her and vanishing.

Far away she could see the ramparts of the fort where Dougie should be. Gugglins were scrambling past her in mindless eagerness to attack the enemy. Boulders and arrows were flying through the sky in both directions from catapults and siege engines and teams of archers. Larger troll-like creatures swung clubs at Ugglins and Gugglins and at one another, combatants disappearing in puffs of smoke when they were mortally wounded. Gorgo was in the midst of it all, laughing fire, joyfully clobbering whatever was in reach. A troll took a swing at him with his club. Gorgo responded by grabbing the troll by the legs and using *him* like a club.

THUD. Another boulder landed right next to Emily, embedding itself into the ground, and Emily knew that she wouldn't just disappear to be endlessly reborn again, like a character in a video game—if she got squashed, she'd *stay* squashed. Not only that, but some of the combatants had noticed her and were running toward her, weapons raised.

"Gorgo!" she shouted. "Get over here!"

Gorgo saw her and leaped, landing next to her with each foot crushing a charging Gugglin. He spun in a circle, sweeping the troll-turned-club around like a scythe cutting wheat, combatants poofing into nonexistence.

"Woohoo!" said Gorgo. "This is so much fun!"

"Gorgo, we have to hurry! We have to get to that fort!"

"But—"

"Now!"

"All right, *fine*." He tossed the troll away over his shoulder, grabbed Emily and tucked her under one arm like a football, extended the other arm, and shouted, "CHARGE!"

Dougie didn't see Gorgo and Emily. Dougie was crying.

"Please let me leave!" he begged.

"No leave! Stay forever!"

"But I don't want to! I want to go home!"

"No home! You king! You stay!"

Dougie began to cry harder. He was scared and tired and hated this game and more than anything just wanted to *stop*.

"Dougie!"

He lifted his head. Who was that? Was that a boy's voice?

"Dougie!" It was a girl's voice this time.

"Over here!" said the boy's voice.

Dougie looked to his right. There was a door he hadn't noticed before — where did that come from? It reminded him of the time his family had stayed in a resort hotel in Oregon — there had been a similar-looking door that led to the hallway on their floor. And in fact, beyond this door there did seem to be a long carpeted hallway, just like in the hotel. More important, there were two children standing next to each other in the doorway, holding hands, a boy and a girl. They were about Emily's age. They looked like twins. They smiled at him.

"Come on, Dougie!" said the girl. "Come play with us!"

"Yes, come play with us!" said the boy. "And you can stay with us forever and ever and e—OW!" said the boy, as the girl gave him a sudden smack on the back of the head.

"Do you have a bathroom?" said Dougie.

The children both laughed. "Of course," said the girl. "Come with us. We'll help you."

They reached out their hands to him.

Dougie took off the crown.

"No! You stay! You king!" said the Ugglins. Dougie

ignored them. Getting off the throne, he walked grate-
fully to the doorway, where Maligno Jr. and Maligna
were waiting for him.

Warriors scattered and turned to vapor as Gorgo rock-
eted across the field, trampling and bulling his way
through anything and everything in his path. A catapult
exploded into splinters. A defensive wall loomed and
suddenly wasn't there. A giant troll raised a giant club
and became a doormat. Emily kept her eyes clamped
shut and prayed she wouldn't be smooshed or set aflame.
She opened them just in time to see a rapidly approach-
ing moat.

"Gorgo, look out for the—" she started, and then
they were airborne, going up and up, and then they
landed on the fort next to the throne.

But when Gorgo put Emily down, the throne was
empty.

"Where is he? Where did he go?" she said, despairing.

All around them the battle continued to rage. "You
queen! You command!" said the Ugglins, pressing
around her, shoving the crown at her.

"Where did he go?" she demanded. "Where is
Dougie? Where is the little boy?"

"Boy no here! *You* here! You command!" they yelled. Gugglins were trying to scale the wall with ladders while Ugglins pushed them back. The fort was shaking from the impact of a battering ram.

"No matter how many I hit, more just keep appearing!" said Gorgo, hurling a Gugglin away.

"You command! You lead!"

"EVERYBODY STOP FIGHTING!" Emily bellowed, and it seemed that her voice rang out across the entire battlefield, rang out from the ground to the sky and from horizon to horizon. And when the reverberations died, all was eerily quiet, the warriors looking at her in astonishment.

"Whoa," said Gorgo.

Then the silence was interrupted by a new sound: a tiny fanfare, as if played by mice.

Emily took the Stone out of her pocket. A chorus started, the voices singing in unison like a Gregorian chant: "You-hoo-hoo-hoooo've go-ooo-ooot a po-oo-oost."

Emily tapped on a small piece of parchment that was undulating insistently. It emerged from within the Stone and expanded quickly to full size, accompanied in rapid order by a large writing quill and a pot of ink. Dipping itself into the ink, the quill moved in a blur across the floating surface of the parchment, sketching a perfect likeness of Maligno Sr.'s face.

"Hello, Emily," said Maligno, the face coming to life like an animated drawing. "You're probably wondering where your delightful brother is."

"He had better be okay," said Emily. "Because if he's not . . ."

"Well! I certainly don't think you're in any position to make threats. But since you asked, he's perfectly safe."

As Maligno spoke, the parchment unfurled farther, and the quill danced over the blank area, and very quickly there was a moving illustration of Dougie, playing with blocks with the Venomüch children.

"As you can see, little Dougie is happily at play with my children. Hopefully nothing untoward will happen. But as you know, children can sometimes be *so* cruel."

The Venomüch children looked directly at Emily and leered, flashing their vicious pointed teeth. Then the girl reached over and started pinching Dougie's arm. Dougie tried to jerk away, alarmed, confused, but she was too strong, and he said, "Ow! OW! Stop! That *hurts!*"

"Dougie!" said Emily, but then the floating ink pot

suddenly overturned on that part of the parchment, covering everything in black.

"Let him go!" said Emily.

"Oh, I think not," said Maligno. "By the way, this is where you say, 'What do you want?'"

"I *know* what you want," said Emily.

"Perfect!" said Maligno, smiling. "Then bring the Stone to us. Your brother for the Stone. That is my offer."

Emily glared at him. She felt beyond tired, beyond frightened, beyond any feeling. Except for one. She felt very, very angry.

Then she heard herself say this: "Here's *my* offer. I'm going to go there, I'm going to get Dougie, and we're going to leave."

"Ah, I see. And we will get . . . ?"

"You will get *nothing*."

Maligno smiled. "Well, now! Why would you have such confidence?"

"Because I'm a Stonemaster," she said, and the moment she spoke, she knew it was right and true, and she felt the Stone tremble as if in a thrill of excitement, felt as if the universe and many universes beyond had heard her declaration, and she waved her hand with contempt, and the parchment ignited and burned away to nothing.

"That," said Gorgo, "was *baaad aaaaa*—"

"Quiet," she ordered. She looked at the Stone. The tiny moon was a mere sliver now, the power nearly gone. Driven by some obscure instinct, Emily held her other hand over the surface of the Stone and thought about the challenge before her, thought about the distance she would need to travel both to the Venomüch realm and then back to her home, thought about what options she might have.

"I have enough TwitCoins, but power might become an issue . . ."

"How can you be so certain?" said Gorgo.

Emily looked at him.

"Right. You're a Stonemaster. Bad *aa*—"

"Shh." She did a series of complicated but rapid taps and swipes. The rough-hewed doors of the Spellevator appeared. Emily regarded the assembled warriors, who were still looking back at her expectantly.

"Okay," she said. "You, you, you, you guys there, you, and you—you're all coming with us."

So she and Gorgo and dozens of Ugglins and Gugglins crowded into the Spellevator.

"What do? What command?" asked the Ugglins and Gugglins.

"Yes," seconded Gorgo. "What command?"

"When these doors open again," said Emily, "you and I are going to find Dougie."

"What we do? What we do?" demanded the Ugglins and Gugglins.

"You guys get out there and wreck things."

It was as good a plan as any.

Too bad it didn't work.

And now we come to the part where Emily meets her terrifying and sad fate.

CHAPTER
TWENTY

S ome children have a treehouse. The Venomüch
children had a tree jail. A wooden-floored, iron-barred
cage in the crook of a fat, twisted, gnarled tree that
looked as if it would mug you if it could move.

The tree jail was in the backyard, high enough that if
you fell, you'd break something. Or die.

The jail had a single occupant. The occupant was weeping tears of despair.

The occupant was Dougie.

He didn't have the energy left to do the sort of full-on
sobbing he'd been doing earlier, when the Venomüch children had shoved him into the cage and slammed the door
on him, laughing and jeering at his pleas and his tears.

They had seemed so friendly when they rescued him

from the Ugglins and Gugglins. He'd been so relieved. They let him use the bathroom (although the skull-shaped toilet was weird), they had given him juice and snacks, and then they had all played together in the yard (although, just like the toilet, the games they suggested had all seemed a bit weird).

Then it had all changed. Without warning, Maligna started pinching him hard and giggling, not pausing even when Dougie started to cry and beg her to stop. The two siblings began roughly pushing him around and slapping his head and yanking his hair while he cowered from them, because they were both much larger than he was and also much stronger than any child he had ever encountered. The girl had picked him up above her head like an Olympic weightlifter and spun him in circles until he thought he was going to be sick.

Then they had suddenly gotten friendly and solicitous again, just like that, and Dougie was confused, and they apologized and said, "Come on, come with us, up this ladder, and we'll play in the treehouse." So he followed them up the hanging ladder to the treehouse, still afraid but thinking that maybe everything was better now. Then the door clanged shut and they were outside and he was inside, and he started sobbing again, and they laughed and went down the ladder and across the yard and disappeared into the mansion.

From the raised vantage point of the jail, Dougie could see that the decorative pond was actually in the shape of a screaming skull. Why did this family like skulls so much? Why was there a small graveyard over in that corner of the yard? Why were teddy bears and dolls hanging in nooses from those branches? Why were those children being so awful to him? Then he realized that the bars of the jail were decorated here and there with grotesque faces of goblins and gargoyles, and when he looked closer, they came to life to snap and snarl at him, so Dougie had screamed and jerked away and ended up sitting in the center of the cell, chin in his hands, each inhalation a ragged gasp.

This was where he was now, feeling scared, bewildered, and miserable, and desperately, *desperately* wanting to go home.

Then Dougie noticed two tall stone doors that had seemingly appeared out of nowhere. He was seeing them from above and slightly to the side. There was nothing in front of or behind them — they were just standing there. Then they spread apart — like elevator doors, he thought — and Dougie screamed in renewed fear. Somehow there were creatures emerging from between the doors, and other than the Venomüch children, they were the last creatures Dougie wanted to see again: Ugglins and Gugglins.

But they paid him no heed. They came stampeding out of the doors, screaming their fierce war cries and waving their weapons, and made a beeline for the mansion, kicking their way through the back door, and then immediately there was a chaotic ruckus from inside, the sounds of things being smashed and overturned and generally Ugglinned and Gugglinned.

Then Dougie screamed again, because something even scarier than the Ugglins and Gugglins had emerged from the doors: a massive demon creature who paused to toss back his head and roar, flames jetting from his mouth.

And then, just before the doors vanished, someone *else* appeared, and Dougie screamed again, but this time he was screaming, "EMILY!"

"Dougie!"

Emily spotted Dougie in the cage as he leaped to his feet and came to the bars.

"Emily! Help me! Get me out of here! OW!"

One of the goblins on the bars of the cage had sunk

its little teeth into Dougie's left thumb. He snatched his hand back and gripped his left fist in his right, curling his body over them protectively.

"Dougie! Hold on! I'm coming! Gorgo, watch my back!"

Emily ran toward the tree, but the hanging rope ladder rolled itself up and out of her reach. She cursed, then put her hands on the trunk, trying to find purchase, but the surface of the bark felt like a cheese grater, as though it would shred her flesh if she tried to grip it.

"Help me!" Dougie was crying. "Emily, get me out of here!"

"I'm coming!" she yelled up to him again. "I'm coming!"

"I want to go home!"

"I'm taking you home, Dougie! I'm here to get you! Gorgo!" she yelled, still facing Dougie. "Help me! Gorgo? Gorgo!"

"Emily . . ." he said.

She turned. Gorgo was facing the house. Acrimina and the two Venomüch children were standing on the back porch casually observing the scene, Acrimina smiling with amusement.

"Hello, Emily," she said.

"You!" said Emily.

Acrimina made a show of looking around as if searching for someone. "Well, *us,* actually."

Maligno Sr. strolled out the door, several squirming Ugglins and Gugglins held by the scruff of their necks in each hand.

"Shoo," he said, and tossed them into the yard, where they scurried to cower behind Gorgo. Maligno leaned back in the doorway and said, "The rest of you! Out!" and clapped his hands once. The remaining Ugglins and Gugglins scampered out to join their brethren.

Maligno turned back to Emily. He smiled.

"Well. At last we meet . . . *Stonemaster.*" His voice was mocking. "So nice of you to come. And to bring the Stone."

"Could we offer you a beverage of some sort?" said Acrimina. "Milk, perhaps? Isn't that what children drink? Or perhaps your own blood, in a chalice?"

"All I want is my brother," said Emily. "I don't want to hurt you."

They laughed at her—the children with their hideous screeching yowl, Acrimina with her cold haughtiness, Maligno saying, "Ha. Ha ha ha. Ha! Ha! Ha!"

"Mama," said Maligna, tugging on Acrimina's sleeve, "can I play with her . . . skull?"

"No fair! You said *I'd* get her skull!" said Maligno Jr.

"Now, now," said Maligno Sr. "There's plenty of skull to go around. We'll split it in half!"

"No one is getting *anyone's* skull," said Gorgo.

"Ah, yes," said Maligno Sr. "Our friend. And your name is . . . ?"

"My name is none of your business," said Gorgo. "Emily, may I?"

"Just hold them off while I rescue Dougie!" She spun back to her brother, craning her neck to look up at him. "Dougie, listen to me. I'm going to get you out of there. Just hold on!"

Gorgo grinned at the Venomüches. "She didn't say *how* to hold you off," he said in a low voice. "Since you did ask, my name is Baelmadeus Gorgostopheles Lacrimagnimum Turpisatos Metuotimo Dolorosum Tenebris Morsitarus. And that's the last thing you're ever going to hear."

Yellow fire danced along his skin. Raising his fists, he advanced on them.

"Wait!" said Acrimina. "Please! Before you . . . hold us off, we have a gift for you."

"A gift?"

"Yes," she said, smiling, and held up the enchanted dagger. "Your freedom."

She tossed the dagger underhand to him. Gorgo's eyes tracked it in what seemed like a slow-motion journey as it cartwheeled toward him in a gentle arc, the jeweled handle and sheath sparkling, and he reached out his hand and caught the dagger neatly. He unsheathed the blade and held it up in front of his face, staring at it in wonder, the flames on his skin extinguished.

Across the lawn, Emily took in a sudden sharp breath and looked up from the Stone. She turned and saw Gorgo goggling at the blade, the Venomüches smiling triumphantly. Right then, Emily understood the trap she had walked into. She was powerless to act, powerless to move, powerless to do anything but watch what was happening, knowing she had failed.

"Free yourself!" intoned Acrimina.

With a sudden fierce joy, Gorgo brought the blade down to the height of his navel, seized something invisible with his other hand, and with a quick sawing motion cut through whatever it was that only he could see.

Emily felt the bond severed and cried out.

"I'm free," he whispered hoarsely. Then, louder: "Free! FREE!"

Then he turned to face her, tossing the dagger aside. He seemed to grow, a shadow outlining his form, as if he were gathering the darkness around him. His teeth were extending too, growing sharper, his eyes blazing. He looked intoxicated with the joy of madness and power, a true demon finally free to reap destruction and terror.

"I'm FREE!" he bellowed, and exhaled a jet of fire toward the sky.

"Devour her!" commanded Maligno. The children leaned forward, excited. In three quick steps Gorgo was across the lawn and upon Emily, seizing her by her arms and lifting her up effortlessly while she stared into his swirling eyes in fear, unable even to scream.

Dougie could scream, though. "No! NO! Emileeeeeee!" Then he turned away, covering his head so he didn't have to witness what was about to happen.

"HA HA HA!" roared Gorgo, and brought Emily up to his mouth, and she knew it was over and she squeezed her eyes shut and—

It's an odd sensation, receiving a gentle kiss on the forehead from a creature like Gorgo.

Emily opened her eyes.

Gorgo winked at her. Then he carefully set her down.

"What are you doing?" demanded Maligno Sr., tromping across the lawn toward them, Acrimina in his wake. "Eat her!"

"Nope," said Gorgo. "I don't eat my friends."

"Friends?" said Maligno. "*Friends?* A creature like you doesn't have any friends!"

Gorgo turned back to Emily. He smiled. "I have at least *one*," he said, and reached out to put a hand gently on her shoulder. "It's over. It's all going to be —AAARRGH!"

Emily leaped back in alarm as Gorgo bellowed in pain, spine arching, clutching his back in agony as he fell to his knees.

"Hee hee hee!" screeched Acrimina, the children joining in. Then Emily saw the dagger in Acrimina's hand, the blade blackened and smoking with Gorgo's blood.

"Gorgo!" screamed Emily.

"Now your *friend* can watch you die!" said Acrimina, raising the blade again. But with a roar, Gorgo swung an enormous arm at her, sending her sailing across the yard, the dagger flying from her hand. It was a blow that would have killed any full-grown man, but Acrimina was much, much stronger than a full-grown man, and she was instantly on her feet again.

"Mama!" shouted the Venomüch children, running to her, but she batted them away impatiently.

"Fools!" she spat.

Gorgo struggled to a standing position and turned to face the Venomüches, and Emily could see the blood seeping from the ugly wound in his lower back. "Gorgo!" she cried again.

"Get Dougie!" rumbled Gorgo over his shoulder to her. "I'll take care of them!"

Maligno Sr. was shaking his head sorrowfully.

"This is such a disappointment," he said to Gorgo. "All we want is the Stone. This could have been so clean and easy. We'd help you, you would help us. But you've gone and ruined it, creature, so now we have to make a great big mess."

"You think you can defeat me?" said Gorgo.

"Oh, no," said Maligno. "Even wounded I'm sure you're more than a match for me. I think it would be dull for you. So I thought perhaps you might enjoy meeting our pet."

He raised a tiny silver whistle to his lips and blew.

There was no sound.

Then there was a lot of sound. The sound of a large section of the high garden wall shattering as a massive creature came bursting through it. Emily shielded her head and ducked to avoid the chunks of stone and plaster that came rocketing inward, some of them striking the cage in the tree jail and denting the bars.

"DAW-GUH-GUH-GUH!" bellowed Gorgo.

Not a dog, or even a dogg with two *g*'s. A doggg. Three *g*'s.

Emily had the briefest moment for the strangest thought: that it was the cutest dog she had ever seen. Fluffy snow white fur, a perfect black nose, soft eyes behind long doggy eyelashes.

Except it was bigger than two elephants, its head the size of a car, and as it came barreling like an unstoppable freight train across the yard toward Gorgo, those soft lovely eyes flared yellow with savage hatred and its jaws opened far wider than should be possible and its murderous teeth were as tall as Emily and there were two rows of them and Gorgo only had time to scream, "Emily, ru—" before *wham*, the doggg was upon him, driving Gorgo backwards to collide with Emily and send her sprawling, the Stone tumbling out of her hands as the wind was knocked out of her. The doggg and Gorgo kept going until Gorgo slammed into the gnarled tree, the impact jarring the cage partially loose from its perch so that it was balanced precariously, Dougie screaming as he tumbled down the now slanted floor and hit the bars.

Gorgo, his back against the tree trunk, was desperately holding the doggg's brutal jaws apart with his hands as the monster tried to eat him. Ugglins and Gugglins were running about in mindless terror. Dougie was still screaming.

Emily, her head spinning, saw the Stone in the grass a few yards away. She reached her hand toward it, and it started to move to her but slowly, as if the Stone was as stunned as she was. Then a booted foot stomped down and trapped it.

"Why, yes! How very kind of you!" said Maligno Sr. "I will take that."

CHAPTER
TWENTY-ONE

Maligno Sr. was bending down to retrieve the Stone from under his hobnailed boot. Emily's head was still buzzing, fuzzy, her breathing still paralyzed by the collision with Gorgo and the ground.

Maligno's hand was an inch from the Stone.

With a wrenching gasp, Emily managed to draw a breath.

"That," she said, "belongs . . . to *me.*" Then, with a mighty effort that made everything go tunnel vision, she willed the Stone to come flying into her hand, Maligno nearly doing a back somersault, as if a carpet had been violently yanked from under his feet.

Emily staggered upright, wobbling, then turned just as

the doggg yanked its head free from Gorgo's grasp and snapped Gorgo up by the midsection.

"Gorgo! No!" Emily screamed, and the doggg shook him, ragdolling him, then hurled him aside to smash an indentation in the garden wall, the impact as loud as an explosion. Gorgo fell to the ground, inert and unmoving. The doggg darted toward him again—how did something so huge move so fast?—but Maligno shouted, "No! The girl! *Kill the girl!*"

The doggg skidded to a stop, turned, and seemed to notice Emily for the first time. His lips curled back in an ugly snarl to reveal his fangs, his growl so low and powerful that Emily could feel the vibrations rattling her teeth and ribs.

There was a scraping noise as the tree jail slid farther down from its perch, instants from plummeting to the ground. Dougie screamed again.

Emily risked a quick glance at the Venomüches. In the brief moment while she had looked away, Maligno Sr. and Acrimina had somehow managed to assemble themselves side by side in lawn chairs, the children sitting obediently at their feet, as if the family were posing for a formal picture. The children were tossing money into a pile, taking bets.

"Twenty says the doggg bites off her head first."

"Thirty says her leg."

Emily turned back to face the doggg. It crouched, gathering itself, eyes narrowing.

"I bet," said Acrimina, "that it swallows her in one gulp."

The doggg charged.

Emily felt that time slowed. She was aware that she was gripping the Stone in one hand, her thumb tracing something over its surface, her lips reciting words she didn't recognize.

The doggg leaped, seeming to fill the whole sky, enormous, monstrous, bearing down on Emily's tiny form the way a tiger might leap upon a defenseless mouse. The beast might have been snarling or roaring, but for Emily all sound was turned off.

From the top of the Stone a blade of crackling white fire ignited, dazzling, terrible in its intensity, and Emily had only the briefest of moments to register that the flaming blade was actually a rolled-up newspaper unconsumed by the blinding fire that danced along its length. Then, as the doggg fell upon her, she swung the flaming newspaper blade in one committed, decisive blow, and then it seemed that she was in the very heart of a fireworks display, sparks starbursting from a thousand points and raining down like flaming diamonds, the doggg disintegrating to nothing.

And before that brilliant curtain of light had settled, Emily turned back to the Venomüches, the newspaper blade extinguished and gone now, and in one smooth motion she brought up the Stone, the Venomüches' image framed in its screen as if she were preparing to capture a photo of them. And *click* she did, except it wasn't the family's *image* that was frozen, it was actually the four of them, trapped, unable to move a muscle, paralyzed in various positions of shock and surprise: hands up or coming up, eyes wide, mouths open.

"Who has the key to that cage," said Emily. Her voice was very quiet and controlled. The only thing the Venomüches could move was their eyes, and she could see them darting nervously back and forth. Particularly Maligna's.

"You," said Emily to her. "You have it. Give it to me."

Emily waved a hand and Maligna was freed from the power of the spell.

"No," she spat. "I won't!"

"Oh, yes, you will," said Emily. "Because if you don't, I'm going to . . ."

What Emily said will not be recorded here. Let's just say that it was wildly inappropriate and completely unacceptable, something that you would never say to anyone, *ever,* unless you were in exactly this sort of situation. Whatever it was, it made Maligna's already pale face blanch even further, her mouth dropping open. Then she scrabbled at a cord around her neck, pulled it over her head, and handed it over to Emily, a complex key hanging from it.

"Thank you. Cheese!" said Emily, and froze Maligna again.

She stomped purposefully across the yard to the tree, the jail shifting even farther as she got close. The floor of the cage was now tilted at the angle of a steep ramp. Dougie was still cowering against the bars at the low end, opposite from the cage door, his weight further encouraging the cage to slide or tumble from the tree.

"Emily!"

"I'm coming, Dougie!"

She could have used the Stone to open the cage, she knew that, but she was now acutely aware that the Stone had very little power in it, and part of her mind was calculating what she would need to get back home. They might just make it, she thought. *Might.*

"You!" she said to the curled-up rope ladder. "Get down here!"

It instantly obeyed. Emily began climbing the ladder,

which was connected to the base of the cage at the door. With a jerk, the cage slid down a few inches on the other side, the floor tilting more, the ladder rising as it did. Emily paused.

"It's going to fall!" said Dougie.

"Dougie," Emily said, speaking as calmly as she could, "I want you to start slowly crawling up toward the door."

"I can't!"

"Try. Keep your body flat on the floor. Just wriggle up toward me."

She kept climbing as she talked. She thought of her science class, the teacher talking about leverage and balance, thought about how her weight on the ladder was helping to keep the cage from falling off the tree on the other side, but the higher she went, the less her weight would count.

"I'm nearly there," she said. Then she heard Dougie cry out and the sound of him sliding back down the slanted floor, and she felt the jolt as he hit the bars again, the cage sliding just a bit farther off its perch.

Emily reached the short platform where the floor extended beyond the front of the cage and eased herself up onto it, holding on to a bar with one hand while trying to keep her weight tilted back and get the key into the lock. Dougie was trembling at the other end of the cage, looking up the slanted floor at her.

"Dougie," she said, and then was interrupted as— *sssshuuck*—the cage slid some more and she held her breath. "Dougie," she continued, "use the bars on the side like a ladder. Climb up toward me, slowly."

"I'm scared!"

"You can do it, Dougie. You can do it."

He started to climb, sniffling as he went.

"Doing great, Dougie," said Emily, trying to turn the key in the lock. "Keep going." *Stupid lock. Come on!* she thought. *Click clunk.* There.

Another complication. The door opened outward, and because of the angle of the cage *outward* also meant *upward*, like an old-fashioned cellar door—and the iron cage door was heavy. Emily pulled on it, partially opening it, and then it slipped out of her grip and slammed shut again. *Wham! Sssshhuuck.* The cage shifted once more. Emily cursed and tried again. The cage seemed to be sliding slowly but steadily now. With a burst of adrenaline Emily managed to throw the door open, and it swung all the way back to clang against the bars, and the cage was definitely sliding, and Emily said, "Hurry, Dougie! As fast as you can!" Dougie laddered his way up the side bars until he reached the front bars, then monkey-barred his way along those until Emily could grab his wrist and pull him free. "Quick! Get on my back!"

He climbed onto her back, clinging for dear life, and Emily started down the swinging rope ladder as fast as she could, rungs starting to rise as the cage slid farther, and then she let go as the cage finally overbalanced and started to fall. Emily and Dougie hit the ground in a heap an instant before the cage crashed into the yard not five feet away from them. The Venomüches, still frozen, watched.

"Are you all right?" Emily said to Dougie, checking him rapidly for injuries.

"I'm okay."

"Good. Stay here."

Only then did she go to Gorgo.

He was lying at the base of the garden wall, eyes shut. As Emily got closer, she could see his wounds and her eyes became hot with tears.

"Oh, Gorgo," she whispered.

His eyes fluttered, then opened. Without moving, he said, "Hey, Snack Food."

She laughed even though she was crying.

"No," he said as she came closer. "Don't touch me. My blood will burn you."

"How do I help you?"

"You can't," he said. He smiled at her. "You defeated a doggg, Emily. You really are a Stonemaster." Then he stiffened in pain.

"Gorgo!"

"Emily, you have to go. You have to leave me."

"No!"

"You're running out of time and the Stone is running out of power. You know it. Take Dougie and go."

"Fine," she said, and touched the Stone. Behind her the doors of the Spellevator materialized. "But you're coming with me." She jabbed a finger at the trembling Ugglins and Gugglins, who were trying to hide behind various frightening lawn ornaments. "You! All of you! Get him in there!"

The last thing Emily saw before the doors slid shut was the Venomüch family shaking off the effect of their spell-induced paralysis.

"You will pay for this, Emily Edelman!" screeched Acrimina.

Emily made a rude gesture.

The Spellevator bucked and rattled as they traveled, the Ugglins and Gugglins clinging to the walls, Dougie clinging to Emily.

Gorgo took up most of the floor space. He had complained the whole time the Ugglins and Gugglins were effortfully dragging him into the Spellevator, telling Emily to leave him behind.

"I'd leave *you*," he had said.

"Uh-huh," she had responded. "Keep going, guys! Heave!"

Now he was silent, eyes closed again, and Emily wasn't sure if he was still alive.

The Spellevator arrived at the midway point, the land of the Ugglins and Gugglins.

"All right, you guys, out!" Emily said when the doors opened.

"No! You come! You queen! You command!"

"OUT!" she bellowed, and they scurried out, the doors closing behind them.

"Dougie, sit down and hold on. I have to help Gorgo."

She went and knelt by Gorgo's head. He didn't move.

"Don't be dead, Gorgo," she whispered.

He groaned. "I'm not. But I will be, and you're a fool for trying to save me."

She held up the Stone, looking at it searchingly.

"Emily . . . Stonemaster . . . put that away. It doesn't have the power left to help me and also get you home. It won't work."

257 ᴖᴖ

"It will, because I'm going to make it work."

"Emily . . ."

She held the Stone, focusing her intention: *how do I save Gorgo, how do I save Gorgo . . .*

There. This one. She touched an apth.

The creature that popped out of the Stone was even smaller than an Ugglin, but with a larger head and giant lemurlike eyes further accentuated by thick glasses. Whatever the creature was, it was wearing a white doctor's coat and carrying a doctor's bag. It took one look at Gorgo and then opened the bag and produced a series of vials and beakers filled with colored liquids and odd gases, one with tiny pink sparks. With a series of rapid pours and shakes and mixings, the creature created a bubbling, smoking cocktail in a shot glass. Then it held up the cocktail to Emily—*cheers!*—and drank it in one gulp. The creature threw everything back into the doctor's bag, saluted, and appeared ready to disappear.

"Wait!" said Emily. "You have to at least *try!*"

The creature sighed, shook its head in resignation, then grabbed something out of the bag.

"Is that a *stapler?*" said Emily. "Don't—" But it was too late, because—*chunk chunk chunk chunk chunk chunk*—the doctor-creature had already commenced a rapid-fire staple job on Gorgo's wounds.

"OW!" howled Gorgo, and the doctor jabbed him with a syringe the size of a bicycle pump, and when Gorgo bellowed at that—"YEOOOUCH!"—the creature took the opportunity to jam a pill the size of a football down Gorgo's throat. Then the creature shoved a bill for services rendered into Emily's hand, saluted once more, and—*pop*—disappeared.

The Spellevator immediately began bucking and rocking more violently than before, throwing Emily to the side.

"Dougie, hold on!" she shouted, then grabbed on to a bench herself.

"You've done it now," rasped Gorgo. "You used the last of the Stone's power. You wasted it on trying to save me! We're not going to make it!"

The turbulence doubled, then doubled again, as though an angry giant had seized the Spellevator and was shaking it up and down and side to side. Emily could hear Dougie screaming, but she felt screamed out. She clung to the railings, trying to catch Dougie when he was bounced into the air. The walls of the Spellevator seemed to be bowing and bending, squeezed and pulled and twisted, and then Emily started seeing flashes of gray light coming in through the seams of the walls as if the strain was starting to pull the sides apart, and then the walls *were* coming apart, separating, and suddenly the walls and ceiling and floor flew away completely and Emily and Dougie and Gorgo were falling, a great roaring in Emily's ears, and she felt Gorgo grab her ankle and he pulled her in tight to his chest next to Dougie, and—

It seemed very quiet. She could hear birds singing and felt a gentle breeze.

She opened her eyes. Blue sky, a few clouds.

She sat up. She had been lying on Gorgo's chest. Dougie was still there, one of Gorgo's arms tucked protectively around him as if Dougie were a teddy bear.

"Dougie," Emily said, and his eyes opened.

"Wha—?" he said, then sat up suddenly, Gorgo's arm flopping limply to the side.

"What happened? Where are we?" asked Dougie, then twisted to look at Gorgo's peaceful face. "Is he . . . ?"

"I don't know," whispered Emily. They both got off Gorgo. Kneeling next to his head, Emily could see the staples in his wounds, which had stopped bleeding. He had a funny smile on his face, as though he was truly at peace.

"He is," whispered Dougie. "He's dead."

"He caught us," said Emily. "He caught us so we'd fall onto him."

Emily could feel the tears streaming down her cheeks. Very gently she reached out a hand and placed it on Gorgo's forehead.

"Oh, Gorgo," she said, "I'm so sorry. I'm so sorry."

Then she closed her eyes, buried her face in her hands, and sobbed. Dougie, not knowing what else to do, sobbed as well.

"Believe me," said a deep, rumbly, and very familiar voice, "you're not *nearly* as sorry as I am. Ow—my back."

CHAPTER
TWENTY-TWO

Angela, her head down, trudged along next to iDougie and iEmily, the three of them just beginning the walk from the school toward the Edelman household.

Emily's parents had looked at Angela very oddly this morning, as if they suspected that something was terribly wrong and their daughter's friend was somehow connected to the trouble. Angela, of course, had no idea about yesterday's visit to the doctor or about Mrs. and Mr. Edelman's intense debate over whether or not to even send the kids to school.

Angela didn't know about any of that. All she knew was that she felt overwhelmed and helpless. The past few days had been a series of close calls and exhausting vigilance and growing fear that Emily would never come back. That thought filled Angela with despair. Once again she pulled the rock out of her pocket and looked at it, as if that would somehow make Emily contact her. But the rock just sat in her palm, rocklike, so Angela shoved it back into her pocket and trudged on.

"Oh, look — it's the freak family."

Good ol' Kristy Meyer, thought Angela, shaking her head, and kept walking.

"I know you all can hear me!" said Kristy from behind her, and then Kristy sped up so she could get in front of the three of them and planted herself there, blocking Angela's path.

"Kristy," said Angela, "what. What do you want? Why can't you just leave us in peace?"

"What did you do to me the other day, you freaks?" said Kristy.

"I don't know what you're talking about."

"You do! You're both freaks! You and Emily both! You played some sort of trick on me before, didn't you! Poisoned me or something, made me pass out."

"Kristy, that's crazy," said Angela. She actually felt bad for Kristy. Seeing iEmily remove her head would be pretty traumatic for anyone.

"I know something weird is going on with you. You're both weirdo freaks! Total weirdos who—"

She was interrupted by a gentle chiming sound. Angela held up a finger.

"I'm really sorry," said Angela, "but I think I have to answer my rock."

Kristy watched with incredulous disdain as Angela pulled a smooth stone out of her pocket, lifted it to her ear as if it was a phone, and said, "Hello?"

Then Angela's face transformed into a huge grin. "Yes!" she shouted, tossed the rock over her shoulder, and grabbed Kristy in a big hug.

"They made it!" said Angela. "They're back!"

Kristy angrily shook herself free of the embrace, pushing Angela away.

"Don't touch me, you loser! What are *you* looking at, you stupid little boy?"

iDougie, who had been observing Kristy with bovine tranquility, continued to do so.

"Stupid idiot," said Kristy. "You're as disgusting and gross as your stupid sister."

Which was precisely when the i-I apth ceased to function.

One moment iDougie and iEmily were standing

there as people, and the next they were dirt statues. And a moment later they crumbled into piles of dark soil.

Angela thought for a second that Kristy was going to faint again. And then, observing her flabbergasted expression, Angela couldn't resist. *"Now* look what you've done!" she said. "You really hurt their feelings!"

"It all looks very peaceful down there," said Gorgo. "Nice place to live."

Emily, Dougie, and Gorgo were standing on the hill that overlooked the town of Clearview. This was where they had landed when the Spellevator had failed. Gorgo had lain in the grass for a bit, groaning in pain and discomfort as he tested each body part for damage, then groaned some more as he got slowly to his feet, Emily and Dougie trying to help.

"Ow. Whatever it is that doctor-thing did, it must have worked. But my everything hurts," he said.

There had been just enough power left in the Stone for Emily to call Angela: "Angela it's Emily I'm almost out of power I got Dougie we're back!" and then the connection had died.

"That was so awesome!" said Dougie now. "The way you were like, *ffsssshoooo!* with that lightning sword, and that big dog was like, *ppshoooo!* And then we were, like, falling, and then . . ."

Dougie had been going on like this since Gorgo's recovery, evidently having made the decision that the whole terrifying experience had, in fact, been totally awesome.

"It was totally awesome!" he said again, for the twelfth time.

"Dougie," said Emily.

"It *was* pretty awesome, though," said Dougie.

"Yes, it was," said Emily, and patted him on the head. She glanced at Gorgo, who was still obviously in pain.

"You all right?"

"Well, I got stabbed in the back with an enchanted blade, chewed up by a doggg, I got staples in me, and then I had these two kids fall on me from however high that was," he said. "So I've been better."

"You saved those two kids' lives," said Emily quietly.

"Yeah, well, only because some Stonemaster used her power to save mine."

He was looking out toward the town as he spoke.

"Thought you were supposed to eat that Stonemaster," said Emily.

"Nah—she didn't look that appetizing," he said.

"Gorgo . . ."

He waved a hand at her. "Yeah, yeah." He seemed embarrassed. Still without looking at her, he said, "I heard you. When we were in my house. I heard what you said to my family." He cleared his throat. "Thanks."

Emily looked at him. He was still staring off at the town below them.

"What?" he said. "I have something in my eye."

"Right." She looked out at the town too, her arm around Dougie's shoulders. "You weren't going to hurt her, were you," she said. "The maiden. When you got trapped in the Stone."

Gorgo sighed. His gaze on the horizon, he said, "There I was, out for a stroll, looking for something evil to do, and there's this dragon. And he's got this maiden. And things aren't looking so good for the maiden. I can't just stand there, right? So I deal with the dragon. Which, believe me, was no minor task." He lifted one arm and pointed to one of his many scars, three claw marks that stretched in ugly lines down his flank.

"So after I convince the dragon to go away, I go to her, and of course she's unconscious. Very traditional maiden, you know, just *has* to faint because it's expected of her. So she's out cold and I'm going to pick her up, and wouldn't you know it, who just happens along? A wizard. Beard, staff, pointy hat, whole thing. And *bam*—suddenly I'm imprisoned in a Stone for several centuries."

"And now you're free."

"Yes, I guess I am."

"So now what?" said Emily.

"So now it's time for me to go."

"Go?"

"I'm pretty beat up, Emily. I've got to go heal. Then, of course, I've got places to wreck, people to eat, evil to do. You know."

She looked at him. "Gorgo, you couldn't do evil if you tried."

"Ouch. You really know how to hurt a guy. Oh, geez. You're not going to hug me, are you?" he said, but it was too late, because she was. His knees, at least.

"C'mon, now," he said, but he leaned down and hugged her back. Carefully. "I think you have something in *your* eye too."

They hugged for a bit longer. When they separated, Emily said, "Am I ever going to see you again?"

"You know how to whistle?"

"Yes."

"Good—I'll swing back some time and you can teach me." Gorgo grinned at her, then took a deep breath. "Ah. Good to be free. Goodbye, Emily Stonemaster."

"Bye, Gorgo," she said, and sniffled.

"Goodbye, Dougie," said Gorgo. "Ach. All the hugging. Stop it with that."

When Dougie finally released his leg, Gorgo waved and began to fade.

"Coooool," said Dougie.

Suddenly Gorgo became a little more solid.

"Listen: you ever need things smashed, you know who to call. Goodbye . . . friend." Then, with another wave, he faded to nothing, leaving just a wisp of smoke that curled in the air and then was carried away on the wind.

Emily wiped at her tears. "Dougie," she said, "let's go home."

When Emily and Dougie walked in the front door, their parents and Hilary were standing there waiting for them with worried, solemn expressions.

"Eek!" said Emily in surprise. "Hi? What are you doing home from work so early?"

"Emily," began Mr. Edelman, "we'd like to talk to—"

"HIIIII!!!" said Dougie, and sprinted forward to hug his parents, nearly tackling them both in his enthusiasm. "I was in this game and there were these Ugglins and Gugglins and then these kids came and there was a monster and it was like, *BOOOOM!* And Emily had this magic sword and there was this magic elevator and . . ."

He continued babbling nonstop at a very high volume while running around, jumping up and down on the sofa, heedlessly knocking over a lamp.

". . . and it was totally cool and awesome and canIhaveasnackI'mhungry!" And he ran into the kitchen.

His parents and Hilary stared after him. There was a smashing noise in the kitchen and then the distinct sound of a milk carton hitting the tile floor, followed by the *glug-glug-glug* of milk pouring out of the container. "Oops! MOM! I spilled something!"

Mrs. Edelman began to laugh, a slightly hysterical titter. Mr. Edelman started to laugh too, also with a manic edge.

"I think—hee hee hee," said Mr. Edelman, "I think he's better."

There was another smash.

The parents began laughing harder.

Then they both turned to Emily and their laughter died and their worried expressions returned.

"Emily," said Mr. Edelman cautiously, "how do you —oh."

The "oh" because Emily had stepped forward to hug

the both of them tightly, an arm around each, her head burrowed against Mr. Edelman.

"Well," said Mrs. Edelman, exchanging a glance with Mr. Edelman, their arms around Emily.

"Are you okay?" said Mr. Edelman after a bit.

"I'm just happy to be home," Emily murmured. Then after a bit more hugging she released them and stepped back. "Okay," she said, "I'm going to go wash up."

They watched her climb the stairs.

"I guess she's better too?" said Mrs. Edelman.

Upstairs, Emily scrubbed and rinsed her face, sighing happily. Then she went into her bedroom and collapsed on the bed, looking up at the ceiling. It wasn't such a bad room after all. She didn't even mind the way the house smelled. It smelled like . . . well, like home, she thought.

Tonight, she figured, she'd charge the Stone in the moonlight and use the apth she found that would make Dougie think everything that had happened was a dream—some apth called Deus Ex Cinema or something. Not that her family would pay any attention to what he was saying, but still. She wondered how it had been with iDougie and iEmily. A bit weird, she guessed, judging by the way her parents had been looking at her.

"Hey."

She sat up. Hilary was standing in her doorway. She had an odd, wary expression on her face.

"Hey," said Emily.

"How are you?" said Hilary. "Are you feeling okay?"

Emily tried to remember the last time Hilary had shown any concern for her.

"Yes—why?" said Emily.

Hilary nodded, but she didn't move. Emily could see her thinking about something. "I'm going to tell you a story," said Hilary.

"A story," said Emily.

"Yes. See, there's this girl, Anna? And she dumps this guy Theo, except she doesn't know that Theo is—hey. Did you just roll your eyes?"

"What?"

"You did! You just rolled your eyes!"

Emily brought her hands up protectively as Hilary came stomping toward her—but instead of hitting her, Hilary grabbed her sister and hugged her fiercely.

"You rolled your eyes!" said Hilary, and it sounded as though she might be crying a bit. "You *rolled your eyes*. You're *you* again."

After a moment Emily hugged Hilary back too.

They sat and hugged each other a bit longer, and then Hilary let her go, stood up, and straightened herself out, wiping at her nose. "Okay, just to be clear—I'm never doing that again," she said, and marched out of the room.

Emily smiled. Hilary was herself again too.

Evan Petersen heard the doorbell ring and sighed. *What now,* he thought, and dragged himself to the front door, anticipating yet another strange turn in his life that would make him doubt his grip on reality.

But when he opened the door, he found a dark-haired, cheery-faced young woman—an attractive woman, he thought—with a clipboard standing on his front step.

"Hi!" she said. "Are you Evan Petersen?"

"Yes?"

"I'm Truly Wilshire from International Insurance Inc.!" she said.

"Oh, Miss Wilshire! How wonderful to meet you! I'm so sorry about the other day on the phone!"

She told him not to worry about it and explained that she was there to discuss the issue of his car, and he invited her in, and soon they were having another wonderful conversation, and then she noticed the mug on his mantelpiece—the mug made by the werewolf, remember?—and exclaimed, "What a lovely mug!"

"You like it?" he asked.

"It's wonderful," she said. She sounded thrilled.

"Well," he said, noting how pleased she seemed, "I've always loved a good piece of pottery!" and her smile grew even warmer and they sat there beaming at each other.

She did not reveal to him that she had always told her friends that her ideal life partner would be kind and gentle and interested in the arts and, above all, *someone who appreciated pottery.*

So let's skip the suspense: the two of them fell madly in love and were soon married and moved to another state and lived as happily ever after as could be reasonably expected.

"You think Gorgo will ever come back?" asked Angela.

"Dunno," said Emily. "It's funny—I miss him. It's weird how you can get used to having a huge carnivorous demon hanging around."

It was after school. She and Angela were sitting on the swings at the school playground, which was empty except for them. It had been a week since Emily had rescued Dougie.

"Check it out," said Angela. Emily followed her gaze. Ms. Hallgren was exiting the school holding an armful of books.

"You know, I was in the library the other day," said

Emily, "and she didn't give me a second glance. Like nothing ever happened."

"Same with me," said Angela. "But that shelf is still there. I found the most amazing book about broccoli."

They watched Ms. Hallgren walk to her car and deposit the books onto the passenger seat. Before she climbed in on her side, there was a moment when she seemed to be regarding the two girls. Emily wasn't sure, because Ms. Hallgren was pretty far away, but she thought she detected a small nod. Then Ms. Hallgren got into the car and drove off.

"Oops. Now look," said Angela.

Kristy Meyer was leaving the school, heading for a fancy car that was waiting by the curb. She climbed in and the car accelerated smoothly away.

"You know what?" said Emily. "I sort of feel sorry for her."

"I guess," said Angela. "But that doesn't mean I trust her."

The first day that Emily was back, she and Angela had been strolling together in the hall before class started and saw Kristy coming toward them. Kristy had turned white and fled in the other direction.

Then a strange thing had happened. Throughout the week, bit by bit, other kids had started saying hello to Emily. Nothing major, no one bursting into song, just a cautiously friendly nod or wave here and there, a bit of small talk in the halls or classrooms. As though Kristy's malevolent influence had been broken, at least enough for some of the braver or friendlier kids to feel as if it was worth the risk to get to know the new girl.

"The thing about Kristy," said Angela, "is that pretty soon she'll recover. And I bet when she does, she'll be meaner than ever."

"Probably," said Emily. "But if there's one thing I've learned, it's that there are scarier things out there than Kristy. Hopefully I'll never have to deal with them again."

Angela was quiet.

"What?" said Emily.

"You're a Stonemaster now, Emily," said Angela.

"I guess so."

"No, you don't guess so. You *know* so."

Emily sighed. "Yeah. Well, I couldn't have done it without you. Thanks, Angela."

"You've already thanked me."

"Thank you again."

Angela smiled. "My pleasure. Just promise that I get to be part of the next adventure."

"As far as I'm concerned, I'm done with adventures."

"You might think you're done with adventures, but I doubt they're done with you."

"No thank you," said Emily. "I think I've had enough excitement for—"

BONG BONG BONG BOOOOONNNNNNG!!!!

The sound was deafening, painful in its intensity, as if they were sitting right next to giant church bells. They both clapped their hands over their ears.

"What is that?" shouted Angela, her voice barely audible over the racket.

Emily pulled the Stone out of her pocket. There were indeed bells clanging on the screen. *Too loud!* she thought. *Too loud!* At once the volume dropped precipitously, as if the bells had been moved a mile away.

"What's going on?" said Emily.

"I think you're getting a call," said Angela.

"I think you're right," said Emily. "But who is it?"

She stared at the Stone. Angela watched her eyebrows go up in surprise.

"What?" said Angela. "Who is it?"

"You're not going to believe this," said Emily.

"Why? What does it say?"

"It says, 'Adventure Calling.'"

"Well, Stonemaster," said Angela, "what are you going to do?"

Emily had a sudden image of herself from what seemed an eternity ago, an angry girl gathering stones on a beach on her twelfth birthday. A girl upset with the world, a girl who hated adventures, with their disruption and discomfort and change. And right then she realized that while she was still Emily, she wasn't *that* Emily.

The Stone was still ringing.

"Are you going to answer, or what?" said Angela.

Their eyes met. A sly smile spread across Angela's face, mirroring the one on Emily's.

"Yes," said Emily. "Yes, I am."